Praise for Dogs Don't Talk

"Heartwarming. Keenly perceptive. A tale of teen travails that will appeal to adults as well as teenagers." – *Kirkus Indie Reviews*

"A funny, warm-hearted and engaging story, with a central character that's reminiscent of Holden Caulfield and fast-moving dialogue that delivers both laughter and serious, touching moments." – *Blue Ink Review*

★ ★ ★ ★ ★ "Fun and quirky, Dogs Don't Talk is a marvelous young adult novel and is highly recommended." – *Jack Magnus, Readers' Favorites*

"May has crafted a book that provides a positive portrayal of high school wrestling, that doesn't require the reader to be knowledgeable about the intricacies of the sport to enjoy it. Although written specifically for young adults, Dogs Don't Talk addresses universal issues beyond wrestling that readers of all ages can appreciate and understand." – *Mark Palmer, InterMat.com*

"Thanks to its sensitive and realistic portrayal of modern family life, Dogs Don't Talk could have a wide variety of readers rooting for Ben, both on and off the mat." – *Foreword Reviews*

Dogs Don't Talk

NANCY MAY

DOGS DON'T TALK

iUniverse books may be ordered through booksellers or by contacting:

iUniverse
1663 Liberty Drive
Bloomington, IN 47403
www.iuniverse.com
1-800-Authors (1-800-288-4677)

Because of the dynamic nature of the Internet, any web addresses or links contained in this book may have changed since publication and may no longer be valid. The views expressed in this work are solely those of the author and do not necessarily reflect the views of the publisher, and the publisher hereby disclaims any responsibility for them.

Any people depicted in stock imagery provided by Thinkstock are models, and such images are being used for illustrative purposes only. Certain stock imagery © Thinkstock.

ISBN: 978-1-4917-5666-9 (sc)
ISBN: 978-1-4917-5668-3 (hc)
ISBN: 978-1-4917-5667-6 (e)

Library of Congress Control Number: 2014922706

Print information available on the last page.

iUniverse rev. date: 11/16/2015

For my family

Acknowledgements

A book is never truly produced by the author alone. This book could not be written without those who gave me encouragement and feedback to press on. Thank you (in no particular order): Nicole Felton, my sisters Barbara and Sheryl, Jean Akins Zybala, BettyJane Gagnon and my husband Larry. Thank you to my editor Dana at iUniverse.

Chapter 1

I think my mother likes the dog better than me, even though I've never pooped on her Oriental carpet, dragged her facedown on a leash because I couldn't resist sniffing the dog's butt that just went by, or even left bales of dog hair all over the house for her to vacuum up.

She gets mad at the dog, don't get me wrong. But after five minutes, she's back to talking baby talk to her and petting her behind the ears.

"Sorry Ah peed on the rug, Momma," Rosie says. *"Ah jes couldn't hold it any longer."*

That's not the dog talking, of course, but my mother talking for Rosie in a Texas drawl. Mom has these kinds of conversations with the dog every day.

"That's okay, Rosie," she tells the dog as she is on her knees, sopping up the latest accident with paper towels. "I should have let you out earlier."

"Ah would've been happy to have taken you for a walk, Momma! Ah'm always happy to do that."

"I know, Rosie." Mom stops cleaning for a brief moment to go over to give the offending mutt a big hug. Rosie lies on the sofa and receives the hug, as a queen deigning to let one of her subjects touch her. It's that bad, how she has Mom wrapped around her paw.

I wish Mom was like that with me. She holds grudges for days when I leave a mess—and by mess I mean I forget to put things

1

away or I don't change the toilet paper roll when it's empty. Or the big one: my room!

"Benjamin, I thought I told you to do something about your room!" she screams from the upstairs landing. I can hear her all the way down into the basement, where I'm trying to concentrate on my PlayStation Call of Duty game.

"I did, Mom," I yell back as I punch the control buttons. "I shut the door. That's what you asked me to do."

"This mess is beyond keeping the door shut! It smells in here. Agh! There's dog poop on your rug!" By this time, she's screaming as though she discovered nuclear waste emitting from my room. "Benjamin! Get up here! Now!"

Okay, so I don't always keep the door to my bedroom shut. But it's not my fault a dog pooped in my room. The dog is her responsibility.

Mom sighs a lot lately, which makes me sigh harder back at her. She's at that age now—middle age, that is—when her assets are no longer her looks. I'm trying to be objective here even though she is my mother, but it's pretty safe to say that she was pretty back in her day. Gorgeous? No, but pretty enough to get by on looks. She still looks good for her age; she's not in great shape, but she's sturdy, where she can walk the dogs a mile or two a couple of times a day. She dyes her hair its original light chestnut brown. She complains that her eyelids are sagging, but not when she's got her eyebrows raised and angry blue eyes are boring into me.

So now her assets lie in this stupid house. Along with her obsessions about dogs and Johnny's autism, she's been obsessed with every house we've lived in, from the one in Oakwood, Texas, to the one in Scarborough, New Jersey, to this latest edition in Adele, Virginia. Through the years, she's spent more time painting, hanging curtains, putting up pictures, and cleaning the house than on anything in which I was ever involved.

As I climb the stairs, she greets me with a roll of paper towels and a spray bottle. She brushes away the strands of hair that fall on her face with the hand that holds the spray bottle. She has that haircut that's short in the back and long in the front, and her hair often falls in her face, creating the effect of one who is constantly being put upon—in other words, her martyr look.

"Be sure to get it all up." She barks her orders. "Use the pet spray, and make sure it soaks in—"

"Okay, Mom, I will!" I say through gritted teeth. "I can't wait to get out of this house!"

"Any time you're ready!" Mom smiles sarcastically.

By this time, Elizabeth has come out of her bedroom, which she has turned into a cocoon for the past couple of months. It's late in the morning, almost noon. I don't hold it against her that she gets up so late; after all, days and nights get mixed up after a few weeks into the summer. Plus, she's got to rest up for her freshman year.

"What's going on?" Elizabeth asks through a yawn, stretching her dancer's arms and legs as she steps into the hallway.

"Rosie pooped in Benjamin's room," Mom says, as though it's my fault.

"She's been doing that a lot lately," Elizabeth says. "Are you all right, Rosie?"

"Mah pelvic flo-ahr isn't what it used to be," Mom says, channeling the dog's thoughts. Mom and Elizabeth have these conversations on a regular basis. It's their strange way of communicating. I find it annoying. The real Rosie is downstairs, lying leisurely in the sunroom with Johnny. That's his usual spot in the house, right off the kitchen but away enough from the rest of the house and, thus, "from too much stimulation."

"What's a pelvic floor?" Elizabeth asks in a loud whisper. "Is that the muscles surrounding your bladder, vagina, and uterus?"

"You got it, sweet thang!" Mom smiles at her as she does her Rosie voice. *"Mah human puppies are so smart!"*

"Rosie obviously sees your room as a place to relieve herself," Mom says, returning her attention to me. "And why wouldn't she?

She probably smells rotting food in here like apple cores, and damp towels that aren't hung up in the bathroom but lying on the floor so that bacteria grows—"

"Okay, Mom, I get the idea!" I snap. Everything she says is true, and I don't have any defense except to say I'll do better next time.

"Smells only a dog could love." She finishes her lecture with a wan smile. "Rosie can't help it. She's a dog."

That seventy-pound brown shepherd mutt is her baby, the fourth child she and Dad wished they had and regretted they never did, being worried that another child would end up autistic like Johnny. I was already born before they found out about Johnny. Elizabeth, my younger sister by two years, turned out okay, but they were pushing their luck. Elizabeth was the longed-for girl. She's like Mom; she loves the dog like it's her sister.

Mom exits downstairs, thank God. She leaves Elizabeth standing in my bedroom doorway. "You need help?" she asks.

"Just get Mom off my back," I say as I press the paper towels into the offending spot. "It's something, isn't it—that she gets on my back all the time and yet dotes on Johnny and Rosie, who do nothing?"

Next thing I know, Mom's yelling at me to come downstairs. "Now!"

When I get down to the kitchen, she and Elizabeth are giving me dirty looks. "How can you think that way?" Mom asks me.

"What way?"

"You said Johnny and Rosie are *useless.*" She looks at me in an accusatory manner.

"I didn't say that! Elizabeth, you're such a tattletale!"

"How can I be a tattletale if you didn't say it?" she asks triumphantly, like a cop who just got the suspect to confess.

"I said Rosie and Johnny don't do any work around here. Besides"—I tilt my head—"Rosie and Johnny don't look too upset." I look over at Rosie and Johnny, who are still in the sunroom.

Rosie is lying on the rug next to the windows, resting her chin on her paw. Johnny is staring out into space, making *oohing* noises.

Mom and Elizabeth look at me as if I just grew a large boil on my face.

"You're complaining about Johnny and Rosie not pulling their weight, huh?" Mom glances at me with a look of disbelief mixed with disappointment. "A dog in her golden years and a boy with autism who does everything he is able to do around here—"

"He sorts silverware and folds his shirts and shorts twenty times before putting them oh so neatly in their *correct* drawers! He's got OCD for God's sake!"

"He uses what he has, Benjamin." Mom shakes her head at me, as though I am still a kid. "And poor you, you're a wrestler, you're an honor student, but ask *you* to do some work around here?" She gives a dramatic roll of the head and eyes, to which I just smirk back at her.

"Damn it, that's not what I meant!" How can I explain that I'd like to get a little of the same positive attention they get without sounding like I'm feeling sorry for myself? "Just forget what I said," I say, as a way of exiting back to the basement.

"Why don't we put Rosie to work, then," Mom counters. "Get the leash. She's taking you for a *long* walk."

"She doesn't like me taking her for walks," I protest. "When I try to take her, she pulls away from me, like she doesn't want to go. She only wants you or Dad to walk her."

"Take charge of her," Mom says, like it's so easy. "This will be good for *you* to teach *me* how to get an animal who's stubborn to be compliant." Before I know it, she gets the leash from the mudroom and hands it to me to put on Rosie.

"Fine." I give her an angry look. "I'm glad to get out of here."

Mom stands in the kitchen with her arms folded. "Make sure you get some treats and plastic bags to pick up her poop."

As if I haven't done enough of that already.

I'm banished from the house, while Elizabeth—I hate her so much sometimes—goes to the fridge to search for a late breakfast and Mom goes over to sit with Johnny to start him up on his iPad autism apps. That's her way of keeping him "engaged"—that and having him listen to music on his iPod.

"Tell me what you want, Johnny," she says in a loud voice. "Use your words."

"Beatles. *Bea-tles!*" He sounds like Frankenstein, with words coming out artificially.

"Okay, Beatles." Mom gets over one hurdle. "Which song do you want to listen to?" Johnny's response comes at a snail's pace. "Johnny, which *song*?"

"Help!" he says finally. *"Help!"*

"Okay, Johnny. *Help! I need somebody.*" Mom sings the first lines of the song as she adjusts his iPod. "Here you go. Good using your words!"

"I can't wait to get out of this damn place," I mutter to myself as I step out the side door by the garage. I head out of the driveway, making a left toward the older part of our neighborhood, where the trees are taller and fuller and there's more shade. After all the hot air I got from my mother, at least I can be cool for the next hour.

Chapter 2

Life is pretty bad when you are jealous of a dog and an autistic kid whose only talents are singing bits of Beatles songs and other songs he's heard on the radio and sitting on the couch all day.

To be honest, I love Rosie too—I mean, as much as a person can have love for a dog, when they remember it is a dog, after all, and not a person. I'm even happy to say I was the one who named her. I was glad Mom picked my choice. The name Rosie means "happy"—you know, as in looking at life through rose-colored glasses—that kind of rosy. And that's exactly what Rosie turned out to be: a dog who is full of energy, eager to please, and happy. That's why everyone loves her—even I do, although I get jealous of her.

But Johnny? He's another story. He's not easy to love, and I'm just being honest. He makes these noises, like grunts and growls, like he's an animal, on top of the singing. Johnny's singing embarrasses me. Mom thinks it's his way of communicating, but she's dreaming.

One time we were in Target—this is so typical—and he started singing this Lynyrd Skynyrd song, "I'm a simpu-ul, ki-ind of ma-an," really loud. And when Johnny sings it, the words take on a whole different meaning.

"Shut up, Johnny!" I snapped at him, and of course that triggered Mom's usual response of "It's okay, Benjamin. People aren't looking."

But of course they stared. "Great, Johnny," I said through gritted teeth. "Tell the world you're retarded!"

"Benjamin!" Mom said angrily. "You know we don't say that word!"

I just wanted to disappear. "I'll go wait in the car," I told her.

"You'll do no such thing!" Mom said. "We're almost finished shopping anyway." When we got back in the car, she tried to be sympathetic toward me. She sat for a few moments without putting the key in the ignition. I sat stoically, knowing this was going to be a "life lesson" moment.

"Benjamin," she started out quietly, "I used to get embarrassed about so many things. I was always afraid of what people thought of me until I took acting classes. Then people told me how good I was at acting, and I took that as a sign that I should follow my dream and become an actress. So I went to New York. At least I met your father there." She smiled wistfully. "But even though I didn't make it as an actress, I learned a valuable lesson: don't let little things embarrass you. And everything Johnny does is little. Okay?" She looked at me with a warm, sympathetic smile before she started the car.

"Sure, Mom," I answered, unconvinced. "I won't let what other people think bother me."

That was years ago. Nothing has changed. I can't help how I think. I care about how people see me.

So far, this summer has just been a series of reminders of just what a loser I am. I don't fit in any better than I did when we had just moved here two years ago, when Dad got a job at the Department of Treasury. He thought it would mean some stability, working for the government. I guess after the stress of working on Wall Street, he could use that.

But for me, everything else in my life is a mess, or to put it more accurately, it's offtrack, like gears on a bicycle when the chain is not in the right cog. I don't fit in anywhere with anyone, especially with girls. It could be because I live in this stupid, nowhere place of Adele, Virginia, a place not close enough to DC to be considered posh, but close enough for people to commute. Adele is a way station; there are a lot of military and government contractors here. There are some locals, but most people leave after a few years. I intend to be one of those people.

But I can't leave here a failure. I need to get a reasonably hot-looking girlfriend and make the guys on the wrestling team respect me. Except for Blake Barker. I don't want him to respect me. I want him to *fear* me. Blake is not a big guy; in fact, he's kind of a little twerp, but he makes up for it by being a big asshole. I hate the guys on the team who use wrestling as a means to make themselves out to be tough guys instead of focusing on the wrestling. Wrestling as a sport needs more respect than that. That's another thing I want to do someday: be a promoter for my sport. Maybe I can be an agent or talent scout for MMA or something.

These are not easy goals, I admit, but they are attainable. When I say "hot-looking girlfriend," I just mean a girl who's attractive enough to make the other guys jealous. I know I don't have what it takes to get a Kate Upton look-alike. I know my limitations, like my round head, which makes me look like Charlie Brown. I hate to admit it, but it's true. Blake first started calling me Roundhead in our freshman year. I tried not to let it show that it bothered me, but I must have failed because he kept calling me that the rest of the year.

That first time he called me Roundhead and Charlie Brown, it came out of the blue. I was beating him pretty badly at practice (I was a good ten pounds on him back then), and that was how he decided to get under my skin, by calling attention to my head. But was it true? Did my head have anything to do with my being unable to get a date?

I wanted to get Mom's opinion in the car ride after practice. The easiest time for us to talk is in her car. She still drives the same Toyota Highlander she and Dad bought in New Jersey almost seven years ago. ("I'll still be driving this car until Rosie's gone," she says.) It's really Rosie's car, with all of her dog hair and bite marks left on the back of the seats. When we first got the car, Rosie was so excited she jumped up in the cargo area and twirled herself around several times, letting everyone know that was her part of the car.

But it's also a place where I can get most of Mom's attention, at least when she's not listening to her talk radio shows.

"Some people say I have a really round head," I told Mom as a way of starting a conversation as we headed back home. "They say it's like a ball!"

"Your head isn't round!" Mom assured me. "It's a handsome head. You remind me of Mikhail Baryshnikov. He has a cute boyish face too, and he was a handsome ballet dancer who was real popular when I was about your age."

"Great. I resemble a ballet dancer. How gay. Thanks, Mom."

"Baryshnikov was a real ladies' man!" she protested. "And he was one of Carrie Bradshaw's boyfriends in *Sex and the City*."

"In other words, a wussy-type guy."

"Benjamin!" Mom acted all offended. "Don't use that word."

"Well, it fits, doesn't it?" I snapped back. "I just don't want to be a nice guy to girls. I don't want girls to think I'm the sensitive type. I want them to respect me too." Then I added, "I also want them to think I'm good-looking."

"If you grew your hair out a little more, it would look really good on you, let people see those blond curly locks of yours," she added.

"I would look like a girl, Mom."

"You'd look cute," she insisted.

"I don't want to look cute," I snapped. "Cute doesn't cut it. I want to look good."

"Well, either way, you're handsome," she said with finality.

"Thanks, Mom," I said. But really, what else would a mother say about her kid? That he's ugly?

The real irony in all of this is Johnny. When he's not making those weird faces—like gritting his teeth, grimacing like he's about to explode, among other contortions—he is really a good-looking guy. Handsome even. He could be mistaken for a member of one of those boy bands with his wavy, dark amber hair, perfectly straight teeth, and impish smile. Every once in a while I catch his deep brown eyes looking at me, as though he can see inside me, into my thoughts and feelings. It doesn't happen often, so it's kind of jarring when it does. It's like we make a connection for a nanosecond, but it doesn't go anywhere.

"Johnny has the most soulful eyes I've ever seen. He's such a beautiful boy," this girl named Kelsey, who was in a youth group Bible study with me, once told me. "When I look into his eyes, I see Jesus."

"Really?" I looked at her with skepticism. "I wouldn't go that far."

"Oh, sure," she countered. "When we love the least of these, as Jesus tells us to do, we become like Him."

"Okay," I replied, as neutrally as I could. How she could compare Johnny with Jesus is a mystery to me. And I hate it when people make these autistic kids to be something more than they really are. To be honest, I don't think Johnny is really thinking about anything. I don't think he has the capacity to. I know that sounds mean, but it's probably true.

Kelsey worked with Johnny at the Buddy Club at school. It's a club where they match normal kids with kids like Johnny. Mostly it's girls who volunteer for the club, and I guess they feel good about helping these kids (who are mostly boys) who are disabled. That's how Johnny's been getting girls ever since sixth grade. Girls would join these kinds of clubs. They would tell the special ed teacher, "I want to work with Johnny. He's so cute!"

But I know what that girl means about his eyes. I wish I had those "soulful" eyes, the kind that girls fall for. As it is, I have greenish/hazel eyes, which are too small in my opinion.

Rosie pulls me out of my thoughts and steers me down a side street—a long side street that leads to a wooded area. *Sure, why not, Rosie,* I think. *We have all the time in the world.*

11

If only getting a hot chick was as easy as going to a shelter and picking one out. You can't just go to a shelter, like you do with dogs, and pick out one—especially not a Kate Upton look-alike.

Rosie's a good-looking mutt, though. Mom and Elizabeth are a little jealous of her even—the way they talk about her!

"Look at those big eyes with black lining, as though she has permanent makeup on!" Elizabeth gushes. "I wish I could have liner like that."

"You could do what Michael Jackson did and tattoo it on your eyelids," I suggest.

"Oh, Benjamin." Mom purses her lips and then smiles. "We really lucked out with her. Feel these floppy dark brown ears that are as soft as crushed velvet. Look at this long, lean athletic body," Mom says, brushing her reddish furry coat.

Elizabeth adds, "Isn't it sweet the way her mouth always looks like she's smiling when her pink tongue is hanging down?"

It's hard to not like Rosie. I can see why Mom (or maybe Johnny, as she claims) picked her out.

But as far as girls go, I'm not desperate. There was this girl in my English class this past year named Melissa who was always striking up conversations with me. She was the kind who was desperate to have a boyfriend. To be blunt, Melissa was fat and dumpy. I'm not into fashion queens, but she could have done herself some favors if she had put on a little makeup and had worn something other than sweatpants and T-shirts.

But I had a soft spot for Melissa. She was into the environment and was president of the Ecology Club. I liked it that she had a cause other than herself in which she was interested. And I suppose I liked her too because, unlike everyone else in the class, she was interested in what I had to say.

"I think it's great that you care so much about current events, Ben," she told me in class one day when I was trying to make a connection between how early American writers like Ralph Waldo Emerson had similar opinions about life and our environment as some Americans do today. "It's a shame our generation doesn't care about things. We need to be more passionate about things that really matter instead of celebrities whose names I won't even mention because they're not worth mentioning. What's wrong with people?"

"Thanks, Melissa, I really appreciate that." And I really did like it that someone else wanted to discuss stuff we were supposed to be discussing, like the meaning of life, stuff like that. I had a hunch that underneath that thick layer of fat was a girl who could be pretty. A girl I would have liked to ask out for a date. So I thought I would drop some hints to get her to fix herself up a little.

"You know, Melissa, my mother volunteers with this dog rescue group," I told her one day before class started. "She takes pictures of dogs and puts their picture up on their website so that maybe they will get adopted."

"Really?" she replied, as if she was hanging on my every word. "I love animals! I have two dogs and a cat."

"Yeah." I trod carefully now. "Well, they found if they take the dog, give him a bath, feed him good food, play with him, walk him so he'll be in good shape, put a bandanna around its neck, you know, make the dog look really nice, then his chances of getting adopted are much higher." I looked at her intently, as if that would give her the subtext of what I was trying to tell her.

"Oh." She nodded blankly, smiling the way Rosie does when she wants more treats. She wasn't able to generalize the concept. To generalize is a special ed concept they use with Johnny. It means he can learn a concept and apply it to different situations.

Unfortunately, Melissa could not apply the concept of taking a bath, eating right, and getting lots of exercise to her own situation. It didn't dawn on her that doing those things might increase her chances of getting a date. It didn't register with her at all. I tried to help her by dropping hints about her looks. I mean, Melissa had potential, so I didn't want to give up so easily.

We had this assignment in English class to do a research paper on a tragic event in US history. "So, Melissa," I started out casually, "I overheard you say you're writing a paper on the Exxon Valdez oil spill disaster."

"You know about the Exxon Valdez, Ben?" she asked excitedly with a broad smile. She seemed so appreciative of my attention— maybe any attention, for that matter.

"Sure. It was one of the worst environmental disasters in US history."

"It sure was"—she nodded—"and yet, you ask anyone about it, and they've never heard about it. Just blank stares. I just don't get people these days!"

So now that I had her attention, I tried to personalize this oil spill. "I think we all could use a cleanup, you know, detox ourselves of all the oil we have in our systems and aren't even aware of it. I mean, think of all the oil on our faces and in our hair and the oil in our foods that are making us fat … uh … I mean, weightier," I said, trying to keep my comments in general terms.

"Definitely," she said, nodding. "Hey, Ben, would you like to go to the library with me? We could do a little research together." She looked at me with wide, hopeful, big brown eyes, just like Rosie does when she's begging us to let her come with us for a ride in the car.

"Uh, well," I stumbled, "I'm doing my paper on the stock market crash, a totally different kind of event." I realized that wasn't a great excuse, so I added, "Maybe after wrestling practice."

"Sure." She smiled hopefully. "When is that over?"

"Uh, sometimes late, around seven, depending on if we have a tournament that week," I replied, and then I let out a sigh of relief when Mrs. Stavers began the class lecture.

Trying to help Melissa with her looks was a lost cause. It's like when I try to play fetch with Rosie. She chases after the ball, grabs it in her mouth, and runs back to me, only to turn away as I try to grab the ball out of her mouth. So Melissa and I are still just "friends," the kind you only know from class and friend on Facebook.

Not that I'm a prize catch either. To be honest, a Kate Upton look-alike would be way out of my league. Well, maybe not *way* out of my league, but it would be a stretch. I know I come across as a bit of a nerd, because I like to read and I'm always raising my hand to discuss things in history class, which makes everyone else groan.

If only I knew how to talk to girls, how to say clever things, risqué things, funny things—anything that would get them interested in me. That's how guys like me, who can't rely on looks, get by: by witty banter. Make them forget about looks. Then once you get past all the talking, you move on to the physical stuff. But I think girls like to be talked to at first. The only exception is if you're a rock star or something. But actually, even they have to say something or sing something. In other words, they have to use words.

Ironically, it doesn't seem to work the other way around. I mean, take Kate Upton (and I'm just using her as a template here—I'm not obsessed with her or anything. I just happen to think she embodies femininity). I don't want to hear her talk. Who cares about what she says or what she thinks? I just like looking at her gorgeous body. But there's the rub: to want a girl for her body or love her for her mind?

As I survey the girls at North Central High, it seems there's no having both. It's probably rare to have both looks and brains anywhere, even in places like New York or Hollywood. But it's especially true here in Adele, Virginia. I think a girl is either too hot for me to handle or too smart and unattractive (like Melissa) for me to want her physically.

I have my upcoming junior year to get myself straightened out. My freshman and sophomore years have been disasters, as far as making my mark in any real way. I'll be turning seventeen pretty soon (October), and I can see my life passing by. I haven't even had a date yet.

I don't know what is wrong with me—whether it is my round head, or my personality (slightly on the geeky side, as I like to play chess), or maybe I am just too picky. Whatever it is, it is making me lonely. And I really don't want to be. I'm really not an introvert. I want people to like me, especially girls.

So I'm trying to figure out my history—how life got to be so difficult for me, why I'm lonely, and why I sometimes feel like I'm going to go crazy. Sometimes I wonder if I really do have some kind of learning disorder or, worse, mental disorder. Whatever is wrong with me, I want to get my life and my thoughts in order. I can't just think about the now. The now is a piece of life, but so is the past. All the pieces need to be put together to get the complete picture.

The sad thing about having a rescue dog is that you will never know the complete history of the dog. I always will wonder what Rosie looked like as a puppy, why she got put in the pound, who her former owners were, who her parents were, what her name was before she became Rosie, what made her so afraid of thunderstorms, and how long she survived on her own. All of those questions can never be answered.

Rosie and I pass by this house with a bunch of kids playing in the sprinkler in the front yard. A kid from the house across the street flies in front of me and Rosie on his tiny bicycle. He can't be more than six, maybe seven. A smile sneaks out of me. Being a kid was fun for the most part, even in Oakwood. We just had the bad luck to live in a neighborhood that wasn't friendly to people who are different.

"Do you remember Oakwood, Rosie?" I ask the dog, as if I half expect an answer. Oakwood, Texas. That's where I figured out I didn't fit in.

Chapter 3

For the first seven years of my life, we lived near Houston, Texas, in this town called Oakwood. Oakwood had lots of big oak trees, and it was always hot and sunny, as though it was always high noon.

Johnny, or rather his autism, cast a big shadow over my early life, because it meant that my parents had to spend a lot of time trying to figure out what was wrong with him, why he wasn't talking and playing with other kids. He looked so normal. If you saw pictures of him as a baby, you'd say he looked as normal as any kid. I would say even up to about six years old, he looked normal. But he couldn't talk like a normal person. He could only say a few phrases and sing songs.

At first, Mom had what psychologists call "denial." She'd convince herself and my father that Johnny was really smart and would look for evidence of this intelligence that no one else saw. To this day, we still have stacks of puzzles that Mom would have Johnny work on. She'd sit on the floor with him, prompting him to put in a piece, and when that was done, another piece.

"Look, Johnny's doing that puzzle!" she'd say as she sat on the floor of our bedroom with him. "He got the right piece in the right place! You can tell he's really thinking about things."

Mom working with Johnny was as big a part of the background of my childhood as the mural of Tom Sawyer and Huckleberry Finn on the bank of the Mississippi that Mom painted on all four of our bedroom walls, and she painted a sky on our ceiling. My mother was really into decorating the house, and this was one project she did that I could appreciate. Our room was surrounded by the flowing blue river, with cattails and small shrubs lining the sandy bank. It was a scene that made me feel calm because of all the blueness, yet it gave me a sense of restlessness too.

What I really liked was that I was a part of that mural. I was Tom Sawyer. The figure of Huckleberry Finn had his back to the viewer, so you really couldn't see his face. He could be anybody.

"Now, keep your back toward me and your face looking out the window," Mom instructed as I sat for what seemed like hours, modeling Tom Sawyer. "Think of looking out and you see a big riverboat."

"Like the picture in the book?" I asked, referring to the abridged version of the classic she'd read to me before going to bed.

"Yes," she answered, concentrating on her painting as much as keeping me focused on the scene we were creating. "Think of wanting to get on that boat and going to lots of adventurous places. Do you like adventures?"

"Yes," I said. "Are we almost finished?"

"In a few minutes," Mom kept saying. But finally, she was finished. "Turn around," she said with a happy sigh.

I stared at it for a few seconds. The face was more angular than mine. The hair was darker. The only thing I recognized that was me was my greenish eyes. "But that doesn't look like me. He's older than me."

"Yes, that'll be you in a few years," Mom said, smiling at me. "You'll be grown up before you know it, ready to go out on your own adventures."

Travis was my first best friend then. He lived a couple of houses down from me on the other side of the street. He was also in the same kindergarten and first grade classes with me. We were both what his mother called towheads. "They look like they could be brothers!" she'd say.

Travis would come over to my house, which was on the cul-de-sac, because he thought my bedroom was a really neat place, and we'd play up in my room on the top bunk of the bunk bed, pretending we were Tom and Huck on a ferryboat. We really didn't know who exactly Tom and Huck were, only that they were friends and they did adventurous stuff together. I was Tom, and he played Huck.

And then there was Mom and Johnny, on the carpeted floor—in the "river"—doing the puzzles. This was how she kept a watch on me and worked with Johnny at the same time.

"Mom, you and Johnny are in the river!" I warned. "You'd better get out before a crocodile gets you! Quick! Swim over here. You can get on the lower deck" (meaning the lower bunk bed that was Johnny's bed).

"That's okay, Benjamin, we're on our raft," she said.

Travis inevitably would ask about Johnny.

"Why is he always doing puzzles?"

"He just does things differently than other kids, Travis," Mom replied.

"He doesn't talk much," Travis pointed out.

"Einstein didn't learn to talk until he was four," Mom answered back, as though a kindergartner would know who Albert Einstein was.

"Who's that?" Travis asked.

"Einstein was a genius," Mom answered. "He was one of the smartest people ever to live. People didn't understand him when he was young either. They thought he was stupid."

"That's a bad word!" Travis said.

"Yes, it is," Mom replied.

The idea that Johnny could be so smart intrigued Travis. Johnny's habit of staring up to the ceiling with a far-off look suddenly was interpreted differently, as if he were looking for divine revelation instead of just being vacuous. Travis took an interest in what Johnny was doing. Johnny held up each puzzle piece like a scientist holds out a specimen in a test tube, staring at it as though it held some kind of secret. Travis wanted to investigate.

Travis and I got off the ferryboat, climbing down the ladder of the bunk bed, and wiggled on our stomachs on the carpet as we pretended to swim over to the pretend raft where Mom and Johnny were working on a puzzle of a picture of knights and a castle. Travis and I started working on the other one.

After Travis and I put in a few pieces of the puzzle, he said, "Hey, let's go to my house." And that's how it usually would go with any interactions with my brother.

The other thing Johnny could do was sing bits of songs we heard while Mom taxied us around to places like Elizabeth's preschool, playgroups, and stores. She had Beatles CDs and played their music a lot. Then one day Johnny started singing, "She loves you, yeah, yeah, yeah." Everyone got so excited.

"And he sings on *key*!" she would brag to Grandma and Grandpa on the phone. They would say how wonderful it was Johnny could sing. My grandparents lived in South Carolina, and we visited them at least twice a year. The one constant in my life has been that we've spent one week every year in Myrtle Beach for my mother's family reunion.

"Maybe he's trying to communicate that way," Grandma would say, and Mom agreed. "Keep encouraging him to sing!"

So we spent our afternoons at speech therapy and occupational therapy. Then there was music therapy and play therapy. Johnny had to learn how to play! Nothing came naturally to him. I just remember saying, "Hey, Mom, can I go in the therapy room? I can show him how to play."

"The therapy room is for kids who don't know how to play," she explained, or at least tried to explain to a five-year-old kid who didn't understand the difference between a kid like Johnny, who had "sensory" issues, and any other ordinary kid. So I would have to wait with Mom in the reception area, where there was one of those wooden block things with all the gadgets on it. You see them in every waiting area, along with the ubiquitous Lego table. None of that compared to what I saw as I peeked through the door going to the therapy room.

It's funny how you can remember things like that from such a young age. I don't remember a lot of what happened back then, but I do remember those therapy places; they were as much a part of my early childhood as going to preschool and kindergarten and eventually grade school. Therapy was just a part of life. Therapy was supposed to fix Johnny. After Johnny was fixed, I could play with him—really play with him. I wanted so much to have a brother I could play with, although I really can't say why. Maybe I just saw other kids playing with their brothers and it made me want to have the same kind of relationship. I don't know. I just know even then, I felt left out of things, as though my childhood was spent living in a waiting room, waiting for my brother to get fixed, and after that, life (and the fun) could begin.

I still remember the dream I had when we lived in that house on the cul-de-sac in Oakwood. I woke up that morning, and Johnny was talking and acting like a normal kid.

"C'mon, Benjamin," he said, "it's Saturday. I'm gonna beat you at Madden today. I'll let you be the Cowboys. I'll be the Giants."

I was so happy to hear him talk that I jumped out of bed and started to go downstairs. I was thinking as I was dreaming all of this, "Johnny, you're … you're … okay!"

"Of course I'm okay, bro!" He got a big grin on his face. "Which is a lot more than you'll be after I'm finished with you!"

I watched him sit in front of the PlayStation screen with his hands on the controller, his fingers manipulating the players in front of him with ease. I just watched in silence. To speak would sink him somehow. It was like that story of Peter walking on water with Jesus, and then Peter realized people don't walk on water and he started to sink. So in the dream, I just stood back and let him talk, and I marveled. I just wanted to hear him speak again. I wanted to play PlayStation with my brother!

I never wanted to hang onto a dream as long as that one. But as I started to approach him, reaching for the other controller to join him in the game, I could feel myself coming out of this dream and I struggled to cling to my normal brother.

"Johnny!" I yelled. "Johnny, come back!"

But normal Johnny was gone, and I opened my eyes to the crappy reality of autistic Johnny. I hated this world! I hated this world because I couldn't fix it. It was broken. It needed batteries. In my childish reasoning, I thought everything could be fixed if you had the right kind of batteries. But there were no batteries that would fix my brother—or me, for that matter.

Would having a brother like this mean I'd spend a lifetime having difficulty communicating with people?

But I can't accept the idea that nothing can be fixed, like my social life, my not having a reasonably hot chick for a girlfriend, my low status on the wrestling team, or Blake Barker calling me Roundhead and Charlie Brown. I don't think I am in denial, at least the way Mom was with Johnny. There has to be hope for me. I'm reasonably normal. I can figure out puzzles. My freaking life is one big puzzle I'm going to solve.

Travis and I liked to play all the same things. When we were in kindergarten, the big thing was the Star Wars movie and all the paraphernalia that came with it. So we would always go outside and play with our Stars Wars spacecraft and action figures, and when we got tired of that, we'd go riding our scooters up and down the street with all the other kids in the neighborhood. It was a nice little street with almost no traffic except during the late afternoon, when people came home from work.

There were these kids in the neighborhood who were a few years older than Travis and me, and they hung around Travis's house because their mother was a good friend of Travis's mother.

The two women would sit outside on fold-out lawn chairs and talk while we played in Travis's front yard.

Johnny would be outside too, but he stood by himself mostly, circling around this big oak tree in Travis's front yard while we played with our Star Wars spaceships. He'd sing these songs by the Beatles, like "I Want to Hold Your Hand" and "She Loves You." I understood him, but he slurred his words.

These kids of Travis's mother's friend were riding up and down the street on their bikes. The oldest was several grades ahead of us, and his younger brother was a year ahead of Travis and me. Johnny started singing louder, which made the oldest one ride up to him. Travis and I were playing in his front yard, near the oak tree.

"You talk better than your brother," this older kid yelled over to me as he sat on his bike, still looking at Johnny, his face all screwed up in a look of derision. (I can't remember his name, but I remember his face. I could sense he was a bully; he had that look of contempt in his eyes. It's the same look Blake Barker has.) "What's wrong with him?"

"He's got something called autism," I said. "It means he has trouble talking."

"Well, tell him to stop making those noises," the kid sneered. "It's bothering me."

The kid kept his eyes on me, as a way of daring me to move or say anything. It was the first time I ever felt threatened by someone just by the tone of his voice and the look in his eyes. Why was he so annoyed by Johnny? I wondered about it but didn't say anything to the kid. I stood there frozen, like a scared rabbit.

Right then—out of nowhere, it seemed—my father walked toward us. He must have gotten off of work early that day. Dad worked at En-Tex, a big energy company in Houston. He was a finance guy and worked long hours.

I felt so relieved by his presence, because I thought the kid wouldn't say any more about Johnny with Dad approaching. My father was the kind of man whose mere presence demanded respect.

I called him sir, and I thought any kid would be intimidated by the sheer presence of him.

"Come on, Travis, let's go ride up to the playground," the kid said. The playground was over on the next block. He looked at me and said, "You can come too, but don't bring your brother."

Dad heard that last bit. "What was that?" he asked the kid in a sharp voice. "What did you say?"

I started to feel really uncomfortable, like I could have peed in my pants. I was grateful for Dad's intervention, but I just wanted to leave and go home. I didn't like confrontations. I still don't.

"We just want to play without him." The kid pointed to Johnny without any sense of guilt about hurting anyone's feelings. He obviously felt no fear of the man to whom he was speaking.

"Well, kid," Dad said with a derisive punch on the word *kid*, "we don't leave anyone out where I'm from. That's called being a jerk. Come on, Benjamin. You, me, and Johnny will go for a walk … up to the park."

Travis's mother saw all of this and started walking toward us. "Is everything all right?" she asked.

"I just had to explain to this child"—Dad jabbed a finger toward the kid still sitting on his bike—"that Benjamin doesn't leave his brother out of things. We don't ostracize people where I'm from." The kid started to realize he was being given a dressing-down and looked like he was somewhat ashamed or at least uncomfortable.

"Oh," Travis's mother said with a look of embarrassment as the kid's mother sauntered up to check out what was going on. She stopped a few yards behind Travis's mother.

"I'm so sorry! I'm sure he didn't mean anything." The kid's mother was just silent the whole time, not offering to apologize or anything. She just looked off, as though she had nothing to do with any of this.

The next thing I saw was the kid and Travis on their bikes, riding toward the playground. It was the first time I had felt lonely and left out. But this episode allowed my Dad to step in and take action.

"Don't worry about those kids, Benjamin," Dad said as he put his reassuring hand on my shoulder. "You know, I have been thinking about this for a while, that it's a good idea for you to start doing some wrestling. I looked up online and found this place called Longhorn Wrestling Club. They have classes for kids as young as five."

"You mean like the stuff they do on WWE?" I asked excitedly.

Dad turned his nose up. "That stuff is phony, Benjamin. It gives the sport of wrestling a bad name. But yes, you'll teach these kids not to mess with you. You will learn to throw 'em down and pin them to the ground."

"You mean like what you used to do?" I beamed. My father had been a wrestler in high school, and he was taking judo classes after work. He was still in pretty good shape physically. Dad had a wrestler's body; he wasn't big, but he was muscular and had a look of confidence to him, and I wanted to have that.

"Yeah, Longhorn has classes for kids your age," he said enthusiastically, "and wrestling is good for all kinds of sports. It will help you when you play tackle football or if you want to wrestle in high school like I did."

"Yeah, I want to do all of that, Dad," I said, holding myself up a little taller. "When can I start?" We headed toward the park with more bounce in our step.

"When we get back home, I'll show you a couple of moves. I'll teach you how to throw other kids to the ground and hold them in a pin." Dad was talking to me as though we were on the same level. All of the hurt feelings I had from being rejected by Travis's other friends vanished.

Dad started me out on the floor as soon as we got home from the park. He was a big believer in wrestling and its abilities to solve problems.

"So, Benjamin," he explained with real enthusiasm in his voice, "the great thing about wrestling is that it teaches you how to subdue your opponent so he can't fight anymore. Watch this."

Then he would demonstrate by holding my arms down, doing a leg sweep that would throw me to the ground, and topping it off with a pin—pretty easy for a grown man to do to a five-year-old.

"You're gonna do that with those kids if they mess with you," he said as he released his hold of my shoulder and let me up.

"But, Dad, they're bigger than me!" I got up as quickly as I could and backed away, not wanting to have him perform a replay.

"Don't worry. The great thing about wrestling is that you will learn to throw guys who are much bigger than you. Here, do this to me."

Then he'd show me how to grab and twist his legs so that he went off balance and fell to the floor. I was pretty impressed with myself!

"Look, Benjamin, you got me!" He smiled.

"You helped me," I protested, sensing a trick.

"No, you threw me! Okay, I did help you out a little, but next time, do that move when I'm not expecting it. Catch me by surprise. That's the key. You catch your opponent by—"

I suddenly went for his arms, held them down at his thighs, and then tapped the back of his legs, which gave way, and he stepped forward, a little off balance. It wasn't enough to put him on the ground, but it was enough to give me an opportunity to kick him again and gain an advantage.

"Good! That's good, Benjamin," he said, his eyes beaming.

Longhorn Wrestling was a top-notch facility where kids competed statewide and some even nationally. The adult classes had some past champions, as well. It made me feel good that I was doing what my father was doing. It made me feel grown-up.

Another way to combat the feelings of insecurity is to get a dog. That was my mother's idea. Travis and I were in first grade by then, and Johnny was in a special class at the same school.

"It's funny," she said as we sat around the table eating, "I was just thinking about how nice it might be to get a dog. I read this article online about how dogs can provide good therapy for kids with autism. They're good protectors."

"A dog might be a good idea," Dad said. He usually went with any idea she had when it came to what we could bring into the house. "I like dogs."

I had never thought much about dogs except when we would watch that Disney movie *Old Yeller*. Mom would always put that video on right before we went to bed. It was one of those slow action movies, the kind they made when she was little. Having *Old Yeller* playing on the little television, in addition to being surrounded by the mural of the Mississippi River with Tom and Huck, made it feel as if Johnny and I had been transferred back into American history. Everything felt cozy and safe, as if we knew what the ending of the story would be, and everything was going to be all right in the end.

I didn't catch the ending of *Old Yeller,* because it would put us right to sleep within half an hour, before "the sad thing" happens, as Mom and Dad would call it. One time Dad was tucking us into bed and Mom called out from downstairs. "Keith, don't put on *Old Yeller* too soon!"

"Why?" Dad asked as he fiddled with the remote.

"You know," Mom answered as she swiftly came into the room. "You don't want to get to that sad part before Old Yeller, you know ..."

"Oh." Dad furrowed his brow and looked serious. "Right." Dad looked up at me on the top bunk and stepped on the first rung to give me a hug. "Good night, son. Don't stay up too late!" He bent down to give Johnny a good-night hug. "Diane, you'll turn off the TV, won't you?"

"What happens at the end?" I sat up, almost hitting my head on the ceiling. I started to get worried about this ending. Everything was supposed to be happy at the end. I didn't want any nightmares.

"In the end"—Mom tucked me in and smiled reassuringly—"he is the father of a cute litter of puppies!" She gave me a pat on the head before getting up and leaving. "Now don't stay up too late!"

So it was decided that a dog would be a good friend for Johnny since he couldn't talk and couldn't make friends with other kids. A dog would be good for me too, because it could protect me against Travis's other friends. But Johnny's autism was the chief reason we got her. Like I said, it was the autism that determined a lot of things back then.

While Dad and I went to wrestling class, Mom took Johnny and Elizabeth to the SPCA to look for a dog. To this day, Mom says it was Johnny who stood next to the kennel with a sign that described the dog as being "one- to two-year-old shepherd mix who loves to play and is very affectionate."

So the next day we all went to the kennel to check out the dog. Rosie kind of looked like Old Yeller, except she had a black muzzle and a reddish-brown coat. Mom originally thought she was part shepherd and part Lab.

"Ah'm 100 percent dawg!" Mom gave her a big hug as she found Rosie's voice. *"And Ah am so glad to have such a wonderful family!"*

That evening at dinner, we sat around the table thinking of names to give her. Dad and Elizabeth came up with names like "Ginger" and "Dora." Then I suggested "Rosie."

"That's it!" Mom said as her face brightened. "That's what she is: Rosie. Good choice, Benjamin." I beamed.

"I get to name the next animal we have!" Elizabeth insisted.

"That's right, Elizabeth, sweetheart," Mom assured her. "You can name the next dog."

"Like we'll get another dog!" I said doubtfully.

"We can get a little dog to keep her company," Elizabeth suggested. Even as a preschooler, she was not shy about stating her opinions.

"Let's just think about this dog for now, sweetheart," Dad said.

Mom would feed Rosie and clean up after her accidents, while I played ball with her. And at night, Rosie's kennel stayed in Johnny's and my room, but I would climb down from my bunk with my blanket and pillow and let Rosie out of her kennel. We used to sing the Old Yeller jingle about our Rosie: "Here, Rosie. Come back, Rosie! The best doggone dog in the West!"

For a while, Travis and I still played together for part of the summer—that is, when he wasn't at the house of his mean friends. When their mother came over to see Travis's mom, they came over, as well, and that meant I was going to be pushed out or picked on. And having Johnny come along with me was like having a ball and chain attached to me.

What I remember about this mother of the bullies was that she always had a wineglass in her hand. She was slender, tanned, with a long nose and a short haircut. Her head was always tilted up, as if some invisible hand was holding it up by the nose. That was just the way her oldest boy held his head, as though he was looking down on everything and everybody. She'd sip on the wine as we played outside. But I could hear some of the things she said.

"Shouldn't she keep a better watch on that kid?" she said a little louder than she probably meant to as she watched Johnny circling around the big oak tree. Travis's mother leaned over her lawn chair and said, "I don't know why she feels like Johnny has to come over just because Benjamin comes over! Why should we have to look after that kid?"

"I know," wailed the other mother. "Can you imagine that goddamned kid getting into my backyard? We've got a pool for God's sake! I don't want to see a dead kid in my pool!"

"Johnny can swim!" I blurted out. They didn't know I could hear them, and I got a sick feeling, as though I suddenly had trouble breathing. They sat there like statues, just staring out with their jaws dropped open. "I have to go home now," I said, breaking out of that uncomfortable scene. I went over to the oak tree and grabbed Johnny by the arm. "Let's go, Johnny."

I didn't see much of Travis after that. Later that summer, my mother found out through some other neighbor about what Travis's mother and that other mother were saying about Johnny.

"I don't want you to play with Travis anymore," she told me in a quiet voice that had a tinge of hurt in it. "He doesn't make good choices in friends. I'm talking about those boys he hangs out with. I think you can have friends from your wrestling class or from church."

"Okay, Mom, I understand," I said, though I really wished I could just have stayed friends with Travis on a part-time basis.

The rest of the summer seemed strange around the neighborhood. Travis never came over to my house again to play Tom and Huck on the riverboat. Johnny, Elizabeth, and I played mostly in our own backyard, with Rosie as our only friend. It seemed as though the whole neighborhood stood with Travis's mother and her friend.

My father came to the rescue again. He got another job, working at a bank in New York City. It turned out the CEO of En-Tex went to jail for insider trading or something. Anyway, En-Tex closed down, and Dad had to find another job. And there was one far away in New York City.

My parents decided we would live in New Jersey, in this little town called Scarborough, which was on the train line so Dad could commute to work.

"It's got great schools there," Dad reassured us, "and there's lots of wrestling programs in New Jersey, Benjamin."

"Not to mention good schools," Mom said.

"And we'll be kind of going back to our old stomping ground, right, baby?" He smiled at Mom, and she returned his smile. New York City is where they met several years ago. Dad grew up in a small town in Missouri, and my mother grew up in South Carolina. Both of them moved to New York after they graduated from college.

Dad wanted to make it big on Wall Street. Mom wanted to be an actress. She even was part of an improvisation group and had an audition for *Saturday Night Live*. She didn't get it, and eventually she gave up the business for "more practical things," as she says.

"I think we can make a happy life there," she said. "Go to the city every once in a while, see a show."

I liked the idea of moving, as it meant I would get a fresh start in this new town. And I would be getting away from those kids with the mean stares and stuck-up noses. I still like Houston, though. I liked Longhorn Wrestling.

I read this short story called "The Lottery" in eighth grade. It was a creepy story about this town that held a lottery every year in June, and being the winner was not a good thing, as the townspeople turned on that one person.

At the end of the story, this lady named Tessie Hutchinson kept telling the townspeople, "It isn't fair. It isn't right." That's how I picture Oakwood. My family won the autism lottery, and the prize was having everyone shun you. That's what stuck with me. "It's not fair. It's not right."

I started to see Johnny as a big liability to my social life. He is the one I still walk twenty feet ahead of just to avoid being associated with him. And who would be my social connection but Rosie, the animal my mother would give words to, the creature with the friendly-looking face and the fluffy fur that made everyone who walked by stop and ask if they could pet her.

"Can I pet your dog?"

Rosie and I have already gone down the street, where it ends with a wooded area where future houses will be built, so we loop back around. The kids are still playing in the front yard. It's getting hot now. I look at my watch, and it's past noon.

"Sure," I tell the kid. He's the same one who passed us on his bike. "She's real friendly."

I get home to see Mom and Elizabeth standing in the family room, which is opened to the kitchen. They are rolling on some paint on the far wall. Mom notices I'm home and turns to look at me.

"What do you think of the color, Benjamin?" Like it really matters.

"It looks fine, very tan," I answer.

"It's called Croissant," Mom says, savoring the word. "It's the perfect color to make the drapes pop."

I've already released Rosie from her leash, and she trots back to the sunroom. Johnny is still sitting there, as though he never got up, his headphones hanging from his ears to his iPod, although I don't hear the faint sound of music. I attempt to make amends for saying he's useless, or whatever it was I said, and sit next to him and put my arm loosely around his shoulder. As if my touch sets something off internally, Johnny starts singing in a flat tone.

"He's a real nowhere man. Sitting in his nowhere land. Making all his nowhere plans ..."

Johnny abruptly stops, as if he is a wound-up music box that needs a few more rotations of the key to keep going. Mom, from the family room, finishes the song up for him.

"... for nobody."

Chapter 4

"Benjamin?" Mom knocks on my bedroom door and opens it before I even get a chance to answer. Same stuff, different day. "Benjamin, you need to get in touch with Mr. Lopez. He said he could use some help with a landscaping project."

"I thought he only hired illegals," I say, still groggy from staying up all night in the "clubhouse," as Dad calls the basement, watching old episodes of *24*. Mr. Lopez has done some landscaping work for us, and Mom took it upon herself to ask if he needed help. My help.

"That's not funny, Benjamin," she says while I brace myself for a sermonette. "We don't need to hire illegals in this country when we have perfectly fine, strong young men such as yourself, eager to do some work."

"Yeah." I yawn.

"Call him today!" she barks.

"I have wrestling practice today," I counter.

She sighs. "I know you have wrestling camp next week, so can you please ask him if you could work for a day? I'm sure—"

"Okay, Mom, I will!" I tell her, a little too sharply.

"Don't raise your voice to me like that!" she snaps before she heads downstairs. *Great, the coast is clear!* I throw the covers off the bed and reach over to get my phone. I may as well get this over with so I can tell Mom I called Mr. Lopez. I get put into his voice mail and leave a message. It's already almost noon. I have to get up to go to practice, which starts at one and ends at four.

Wrestling has been something I've looked forward to since those days in Oakwood. Wrestling is all about being in the moment; it's a sport where everything is all up to you, and if you get good enough, you control the mat. It feels good being in control.

But at North Central High, wrestling is not fun. It's sheer drudgery. Coach Garlin—or Coach "G," as he is known—is eaten up with winning states. He, or rather the team, has consistently been in the top three in the state for the past five years—except last year, when we finished in fourth place. That was a big deal, and Coach G was livid. I guess that's the downside of always being at the top—the pressure to stay there. Even in the summer, he yells at us, as though it is wrestling season.

It's hot in the wrestling room even though it's air-conditioned, and there's a pervasive smell of sweat. Because it is summer, there are only about fifteen of us here; usually we have about forty guys during the school year. But I like Coach G to see that I'm serious, that I want to be the starter for the 140-pound weight class.

My usual rival, Mike Duhon, is not here. He must be on vacation or working. Those are the only excuses the coach will accept and, of course, only in the summer. But Mike is pretty good, and it's always a toss-up as to who is better, Mike or me. We're pretty evenly matched.

But it feels good to be in with a group of mostly top high school wrestlers and to be able to keep competitive. If I had to rate myself as an athlete on a scale of one to ten, ten being professional quality, I would say I am a five or six. I could get a scholarship at a decent school, maybe not UVA or Virginia Tech, but maybe George Mason or even VMI.

We start with a little grappling, and I'm paired with J. T., who's a good ten pounds on me. I like J. T. although he and I don't seem to have much in common. He's good-looking in that dumb jock kind of way, with bulging muscles; a chiseled face; big, light blue eyes; and blondish hair cut close to the head, kind of like a beefed-up Ken doll.

We get to the live wrestling part of practice, where we go one-on-one, starting usually with the lighter-weight guys. That's the time when a wrestler can sit back against the gym wall, drink some water, and wait for his turn. Most of the guys pull out their phones and text or play games. I pull out my book, *Better Chess in Nine Steps.*

Live wrestling is wrestling full-out, hard, like it's a competition. Blake Barker goes first against this little freshman. What Blake lacks in size he makes up by being the biggest weasel on the team. He literally looks like a weasel with beady eyes and a pointy nose that always seems to twitch. And he's sneaky.

He wastes no time with this new kid, and as soon as the coach whistles, he grabs the kid by the arms and attempts a takedown. But this kid counters him by turning his back to Blake, digging his hip into him, and scores a takedown.

Blake gets all mad, and I watch to see if he tries any dirty tricks like he did with me. He gets up off the mat and turns to the kid.

"Come on," he says to the kid, motioning with his arms, "let's see you try that again." So the new kid obliges. It's like lather, rinse, repeat. Blake is down. I smile at his humiliation—that is, until I see him punch the kid in the gut when the coach's head is turned. The poor kid is too shocked and winded to say anything.

"Next up," Coach G yells. I won't be up for another couple matches, so I go back to reading. Or at least I try to.

Blake's towel and gym bag are a few feet away from me. While wiping off his defeat, he takes a jab at me.

"You're reading a book, Charlie Brown?" He laughs derisively. "About chess?" I don't know what's funnier to him, that I have a book or that it's about chess. "But you're not an egghead. You're a roundhead."

"It's called reading, Blake," I retort, although I really want to tell him he's a shithead. "You should really try it sometime." But Blake's already gone before I even say his name.

"We don't do a lot of reading around here, Ben," J. T. tells me, as if he's giving me pointers on how to fit in. "We're doers, not readers." He takes another swig of bottled water and stares out at the opposite wall of the gym.

"Thanks, J. T., I appreciate the heads-up," I tell him. I've been a part of the team as long as he has, but I'm still having trouble fitting in. I close the book and put it back in my gym bag. I wish there was someone on the team who liked to read. I don't mean to sound like a snob, but why do they have to behave like dumb jocks?

I guess I enjoy reading more than the average kid. It is something besides sports that has kept me sane. I am always looking for a good book. I really got into reading when I was in the sixth grade. I like the Margaret Peterson Haddix books *Among the Hidden* and *Among the Brave.* They are of that genre of books about disturbing places with authoritarian governments. I was the first among my whole class—and I mean the entire sixth grade—to read *The Hunger Games.* In a way, I was a trendsetter.

But does being on a wrestling team mean you have to act illiterate? Even back then, I got teased for reading. Scarborough, New Jersey, had a reputation for having one of the best schools in the country, so you'd think being a reader would be a good thing—but not if you're on the middle school wrestling team.

"I found this book at Barnes and Noble," Mom told me as we rode back home after wrestling practice. "It got great reviews, and it is the number one book among seventh graders." She gave me a copy of *Twilight.* Normally, I liked to pick out my own books, but I thought I'd humor her and give it a try. "Thanks, Mom," I said.

I took the book and started reading the back cover. It seemed okay, full of vampires and werewolves. It's not my kind of thing, but once I start a book, I hate to not finish it. So I thought I could get into it. I put it in my backpack so that I could kill some time in between school and afternoon wrestling practice. On this day, there was a substitute in English lit class, and she told us to spend class time reading a book. So I pulled out *Twilight*, not giving it much thought.

I looked up and noticed the girl who sat at the desk to my left was staring at the cover of my book. Since the beginning of the school year, I kind of had a crush on her. She was a light-skinned Indian and had the prettiest dark eyes I've ever seen, not to mention beautiful straight teeth and an inviting smile. She looked at me and smiled.

"What chapter are you on?" She looked at me, still smiling, as she held up her copy of the book.

"I'm just getting started," I reply, smiling back. "I'm only on chapter two. She's just started going to this new school."

"Yeah." She smiled. "I love how it builds up in an ominous way, don't you think? I can't put it down," she gushed.

"Yeah, it looks like it's going to be a good story." I smiled back. It was nice to have a pleasant conversation with a girl. She really seemed into the book. She told me several of her friends were reading it.

"Maybe we can get together for a book club," she suggested.

"Sounds like fun," I said, smiling in spite of trying to maintain a look of seriousness. I wanted to give an air of sophistication, and I decided my smile wasn't sophisticated. When I smiled I always came off looking goofy, like a third grader's school picture. She must have thought I was acting a little weird, nodding my head, alternating my expression from goofy smile to serious furrowed brows.

After school I went to the locker room to dress out for wrestling practice. I opened my backpack and *Twilight,* which was the last thing I stuck in there, fell out.

"Hey, Benny. What's this?" This kid Danny Abruzio takes the book, as though he had caught me with something worse than drugs. "*Twilight*? Benny, seriously. You're reading *Twilight*? Hey, Vinny! Guess what Benny's reading!"

It was like the whole locker room exploded in laughter.

"That's a girls' book!"

How could I not have known that? This was important information for a middle schoolboy to know, and I didn't know it. I could spout off any trivial information, like who the vice president or governor was, but who cared about that? It's not knowing things like *Twilight* was a girls' book that made me an outcast socially, way back in middle school.

From then on, I was known as "Twilight" by the team. Even the coach called me that.

"C'mon, Twilight," he teased me during practice. "Get his leg. Don't let the werewolf escape!"

For a split second, I lost concentration and the kid I was live wrestling with managed to get his leg around where I couldn't grab it. I got really angry because I let the teasing get to me. I got so angry at this point I just bulldozed the kid right out of bounds.

"Hey, take it easy," the other kid said.

"C'mon, you want to call me Twilight too? Go ahead." I motion for him to come at me. "I'll show you what I do to guys who try to be funny."

I don't know why I said all that to the kid, because he never called me that. It was the coach who said it to make me mad. I tried not to let on that it bothered me, because if they knew how much it bothered me, it would just egg them on. I decided to just let it fuel my adrenaline and make me wrestle harder.

Okay, the *Twilight* episode is a bad example, I know. I deserved to have gotten a hard time about reading such a dumb book. At least some of the guys on the middle school team back in New Jersey liked to read fantasy or graphic books. But these guys at North Central don't read anything: thrillers, mysteries, war stories. Nothing.

It's my turn on the mat. I get up to wrestle with J. T., and even though he's bigger, I'm faster and I'm able to get hold of his leg and get him off balance. The trick with J. T. is holding him down. I almost have him in a pin, but he manages to turn over onto his stomach. Then time runs out. I only score a near-fall on him, but still a win.

"Almost got a pin, Ben!" J. T. smiles with no sense of frustration at having lost. "But you didn't!" I wish I could be like J. T. Nothing ever bothers him.

Practice mercifully ends, and I drive home. I love driving. Nothing makes me feel freer than getting behind the wheel, turning on *my* radio stations—no talk radio crap—and taking off, even if taking off is no more than a few miles to the school.

Then some good news greets me when I get home. Dad is already home and tells me he wants to meet up with some of his old business associates in New York on Friday.

"How about let's make it a road trip, Benjamin? We could stop in Scarborough and maybe you could see Brian and Seth."

I light up. "Yeah, that sounds good. Let me text them and see if they'll be around."

"When is wrestling practice on Friday?" Dad asks, making sure his number one priority doesn't get short shrift.

"Dad, we never have practice on Fridays in the summers." I'm starting to get the idea he's backpedaling.

He looks a little doubtful about the logistics. "When does wrestling camp start?"

"Late Sunday," I tell him, trying to minimize any conflicts in scheduling. "We don't have to check in until late Sunday."

Dad thinks for a minute. Everything takes a backseat to wrestling. "You can't miss any workouts." He scratches his chin. "How about let's leave real early on Sunday. We'll make it work."

"That sounds great." I let out a big sigh of relief. "Thanks, Dad!" I head upstairs to shower and text Brian and Seth.

Brian and Seth are my wingmen. I know that sounds a little cocky, but that's what it's always been like ever since third grade. Even back then I was interested in girls. Brian and Seth, not so much. Even now, when I call them up or text them and ask what's going on, it's never about girls. Both of them are so shy about girls, they've never even asked a girl out. At least I've tried … twice. But that's what makes them great as wingmen. No competition. No one to make me feel like a loser.

I sure could use a break from all that.

"That sounds like a plan, Dad," I say.

Chapter 5

Dad is a lot like me; he's restless. He likes to get out of the house as much as my mother likes to stay home. As soon as he gets home from work, it's like he wants to escape. So he grabs Rosie's leash, puts it on her, and goes out for a walk.

"I've been sitting in front of a computer all day," he says, as if he owes Mom an explanation. "I just need to get out and get some fresh air."

My father is of average height, but he has an imposing presence. His hair is thinning and he still has a somewhat chiseled face, even though his jawline has that middle-age sag. His eyes always seem to be squinting, as though he is constantly on the lookout for signs of trouble.

Dad is from Texas, and maybe in another time he would have been the kind of man who owned his own ranch, the kind of man who went off on horseback and stayed away for long lengths of time. As it is, he works in an office. When he worked in New York and Texas, he worked on a trading desk, which was a big room with dozens of computer monitors sitting on top of long rows of tables. Now that he's with the Treasury Department, he has a little cubicle.

They are complete opposites in that way. My mother is a homebody, a woman "who works in the home," to put it in the politically correct way. But she likes it. She mows the lawn, fixes things when they need repairing, like the plumbing, cooks, and cleans—the usual stuff. She could stay at home all day if she didn't have kids to chauffer around and Rosie to take to the neighborhood park to get her morning walk and play with other dogs at the "bark park."

I wish I could have known the fun person my mother was when she was young, when she still had dreams.

With pursed lips, Mom is listening to Dad talk about going on a road trip. "I thought it would be a good idea to have Benjamin work a little this weekend. He has wrestling camp next week so he won't be able to earn a little money. Then—"

"Oh, you mean with the landscape guy?" Dad asks dismissively. "He can do that another weekend. He'll always need someone to mow or whatever."

Mom clearly looks put out. It's a regular feature in their tug-of-war with my life. Mom is always getting on my case to clean up and get a job. She constantly nags me about learning to become more independent.

"You don't want to end up being one of those guys who can't cook or clean up after themselves," she tells me. "And your wife will not want to pick up after you!" She looks at me with raised eyebrows.

"Like I'll ever get married," I snort.

"Of course you will," she says. She wants me to get out of the house, "be your own man." She couldn't wait for me to get my license so I could "get a job, be more independent." I have to admit I'm glad she pushed me to get my driver's license. I don't know why I put off taking the test for the learner's permit. Maybe it was because I knew subconsciously what I was in for. It was torture going through the process—having Mom sitting in the passenger's seat clutching the armrest on the door, yelling "Slow down" and "Stop!" every hundred feet.

"I'm so glad you finally got your license!" Mom gave me a big hug when I showed her my certificate from driver's ed stating that

I passed the driving test. "I don't know which was harder, giving birth to you or giving you your driver's license."

"You didn't give me a driver's license, Mom. I did that myself!" And to bring that point home, I added, "Maybe it would have been easier if you had just relaxed a little."

"We did it together," she beamed at me. "Remember, I was the one who pushed you. Both times!"

"Well, thanks, Mom!" I said, wanting to bring this conversation to a close.

But that's one of the advantages of having "an early birth date," meaning I am one of the oldest in my class. I'll get to drive Brian and Seth around. I'll have my own wheels.

"Can I borrow the car one night so Brian and Seth and I can go out?" I ask just to make sure.

"Sure," Dad says. "Have a good time."

Dad always focuses on the bigger picture: my wrestling and grades, and getting into a decent college. My wrestling could mean a scholarship or at least a boost on any college application. He also knows how important it is to have fun and see old friends.

"Come on, it'll be fun." He puts his arm around Mom. "We can all go.

Elizabeth would like to see her friends too, I bet."

"Elizabeth has dance workshop this weekend, starting Friday," Mom counters. "Plus, what would we do with Rosie?"

Then Elizabeth interjects. "I don't have to go to that workshop, Mom. I can do a dance camp in August." Elizabeth has been taking dance classes ever since she was six. It used to be all she wanted to talk about. But lately, she wants to get out more, see people, do all the things she missed out on. "Can I go too, please?" she pleads.

Elizabeth's best friend is Anna, whom she met in Girl Scouts back in Scarborough. Anna is the sister she never had. Elizabeth hasn't made any really close friends since we moved to Adele two years ago, although she's on the middle school's dance team. Like me, Adele doesn't feel like home for her either, but at least she has some acquaintances.

"Well, let's think about this." Dad bides his time. "We could put her in a kennel here or look for a pet-friendly hotel. I think there's one in Scarborough. I could drop Elizabeth off at Anna's house. Would you like that, Elizabeth?" She nods enthusiastically. That leaves Mom alone with Johnny and Rosie for the weekend.

But Mom is a regular fun vacuum. Any thought of doing something just for pleasure's sake, and she sucks it up and puts a dour look on her face.

"Well, you'll be going to see your business associates, Elizabeth has Anna, Benjamin has Brian and Seth. Somebody will have to stay with Johnny and Rosie. Why don't I just stay here with them?"

"Are you sure that's okay, Diane?" Dad looks unsure. "You and Johnny staying here with the dog by yourself?" Mom nods, letting out more than a hint of martyrdom.

"Go ahead, y'all have fun," she says.

"I'll make sure Benjamin gets some work in this summer," Dad reassures her, to which she lets out a sigh loud enough to register her displeasure but quiet enough to cease any more discussion with Dad.

I text Brian and Seth to ask if they'll be in town. Of course, everything hinges on that. Seth texts me back and asks me to Skype him in about five minutes.

"Sure," I text back. So I go in the study, the only room in the house other than the bedrooms where you can close the doors— the best place to Skype.

"It'll be great to see you, Ben," Seth tells me. "You look good, man. Shaving yet?"

I laugh. "A little. How 'bout you?"

"Just around the mustache area and the chin." He grins.

The picture is a little blurry, so I can't make out too much except that Seth looks like his face has rid itself of some baby fat.

He looks more mature than he did six months ago when we last Skyped. He and I mostly text or instant message each other—more so than with Brian, who seems more distant lately, and not only by geography.

"Yeah, Brian is lifeguarding now," Seth says. "I don't see him around much. You know how he is, kind of shy, or maybe aloof is a better word."

"Yeah, I know what you mean about Brian," I say as I look at myself in the smaller screen at the top left of the big screen. "He's always been that way. I think it's because he was always the shortest kid in the class and felt left behind."

"Well, I think you'll be surprised to see him now." Seth raised his eyes, as if surprised himself. "He's taller than me!"

"Wow," I say.

"But you know Brian." Seth shakes his head while looking at his own picture instead of the Skype lens and, thus, at me. "He's still insecure about stuff."

"You mean girls?"

"Oh, Ben, there you go again!" He shakes his head and smiles.

"Well, what else would he be insecure about?"

"Well, I dunno, he's just the shy type, I guess. Doesn't say much." Then Seth asks me if I go out on dates.

"Well, not really," I confess. "But we've got to go out and try. I mean, you're a nice-looking guy, Seth. You shouldn't have any trouble getting a girl."

"Girls take too much energy to think about." Seth dismisses me.

"What do you mean?" I ask, exasperated. "All I'm suggesting is talking to girls."

"Yeah, I know," Seth says, already sounding tongue-tied at the thought of talking to a girl. "I can't think about what I would say to a girl. I've got to concentrate on my grades and getting into college. That's why I'm doing some community volunteer work, some odd jobs here and there, doing a little prep work for school."

Oh, great, I'm thinking. *Brian is working, and Seth is volunteering. Two things Mom is always getting on my case about doing.*

"Well, we all have time to go out on Saturday, I hope," I half plead with him.

"Sure, it'll be great seeing you, Ben!" And he adds with a laugh, "And it'll be great seeing Brian too!"

We talk for a few more minutes about baseball. He's a big Phillies fan, but we both have our fantasy teams so we discuss the merits of each player. Afterward I get a text from Brian.

"I have to lifeguard from noon to 5."

I text him back.

"Seth and I are going out Saturday night. Why don't you come along?"

"Sure. Ok."

If it were just about playing video games, Brian would be all excited, but ask him to go places and he freezes up. They both have a little social anxiety. So do I, but as the saying goes, "feel the fear and do it anyway." That's how I get through a lot of my wrestling matches.

Seth and Brian may not be the most confident guys to go "on the prowl" with, but it's good to have friends come along. It's easier to meet girls when you approach them in a pack. At least, it seems that way. I'm no expert.

We pack up the night before and hit the road at about nine thirty in the morning, just after most of the rush hour traffic on I-95 has passed. Elizabeth offers to sit in the middle row of the Tahoe. It's our long-distance traveling vehicle. She puts on her headphones and listens to music, while Dad and I sit up front. He's got satellite radio, and we listen to a little sports talk, the only talk radio I like.

"Ready for the weekend?" Dad asks enthusiastically. "Who knows, Benjamin"—Dad has a big grin on his face—"maybe you'll run into Tamara!"

I punch him in the arm, but he doesn't let up.

"Tamara and Ben, sitting in a tree …"

I punch him even harder, but I can't help but smile.

"Hey, watch it! I'm driving!" He gets serious for a second and then laughs. He still teases me about Tamara.

Chapter 6

Brian and I became best friends in third grade. That relationship has remained pretty much intact, though, to be honest, we mostly connect through sports and playing video games. Whenever I start talking about stuff like girls or anything too touchy-feely, Brian wants to change the subject.

Third grade was the first year I had a good time in school. Mr. Green was our teacher, and it was great having a man for a teacher. He was also the soccer coach for the high school, and he liked all kinds of sports, which made his class fun.

Brian sat across from me in this cluster of four desks pushed together. The other two in our group were Aditya and Tamara. Aditya lived in my neighborhood and rode the same bus as me. Tamara's desk was to the right of mine. Having Tamara sitting next to me was annoying because she was so nosy. It would have been better if we could have switched places, because I'm a southpaw, and if she had sat to my left, it would have taken more effort to check out what I was writing.

"Ben, what are you writing about in your journal?" she'd ask in that rather uppity tone she'd use. Tamara carried herself off as another Hermione Granger, who prided herself on being able to keep up with the boys in her group, as well as being a big show-off. "I'm writing about my trip to New York City and getting to go on the big Exchange floor, you know, where they trade stocks?"

"I know what stocks are, Tamara," I said, rather annoyed. "My father's in the financial business."

"Well," she continued, "I'm sure you have something thought provoking to put down. Oh, wow, soldiers in Iraq. Now that's interesting!"

"It's supposed to be personal, Tamara," I said defensively. Brian smiled as he leaned back in his chair and stretched.

"I'm writing about the Mets. They're the best baseball team!"

"You mean they *were* the best, millions of years ago!" I answered. "Everyone knows the Yankees are the all-time best."

"Everybody's a Yankees fan," Brian said. "There's no fun it that!"

That was the start of our friendship. It was based on the love of baseball. We ended up playing on the same team that spring. Brian was a little kid back then, the shortest kid in the class. He also had a tiny, high-pitched voice which made him sound younger than everyone else, so the other kids tended to not take him seriously. But that's what made me like him. He was different. He was like an underdog, and I thought of myself as a fellow underdog.

I met Seth soon after. He lived in Brian's neighborhood and ended up on our team. Seth and Brian were pretty good ballplayers. I liked baseball too, though it was something I had to work harder at. Baseball required different skills, more hand–eye coordination. I wanted to be a pitcher, although I was not good at all at first. But that didn't stop me from trying.

So I practiced every day. Dad got me a pitching net and put it out in the yard, and after school I'd be out there pitching that ball. I didn't get on the first string that spring season in third grade. But baseball was fun. The dugout was fun, and Brian, Seth, and I would talk about our favorite teams and all the stats.

But one day, it got a little personal. "You know who else likes you?"

"Who?"

He snorted and blurted out, "Tamara."

"No, not Tamara!"

"Everyone knows she likes you!"

"Really?" I looked at him doubtfully but thought this was an interesting bit of knowledge.

"That's what Attiya says. I'm telling you, Benny," Brian said, looking at the pitcher, "she really likes you!"

"Yeah, she's good friends with a girl in my class," Seth added. "This girl sits near me, and I heard her talking about the boys they like. It's true."

"How can you tell?" I must have not developed this girl radar that other guys, even Brian, had that let them know a girl liked them.

"You can tell by the way she's always getting on your case about something. You know, kind of like a wife!" He snorts at the word *wife*.

"Get out!" I chuckled and gave him an elbow.

"Well, it's true!"

If Tamara liked me, she had a weird way of showing it. Once she and I had a run-in when she told Mr. Green that I wrote something in my writing journal that she thought was "inappropriate." I got mad at her for looking at my journal and told her off. "I'm so sorry I hurt your feelings, Benny," she later wrote on construction paper. She drew a picture with some crayons of a girl and marked it "Me" and another figure right next to it that she marked "You." Then she drew a heart between them.

I couldn't believe Tamara liked me, but to this day Brian insists she liked me. I'd never know for sure, as Tamara moved away the next year.

It's kind of nice to know that at one time in my life, a girl liked me, especially one as cute as Tamara. I admit she was a cute girl, the kind who would probably grow up to be a good-looking girl. If I ran into Tamara today, I wonder if I'd have a chance with her.

We get to Scarborough in the late afternoon, and Dad drops Elizabeth off at Anna's house first, and then we check into a hotel near the train station.

"Tomorrow you can have the car all day," Dad tells me as we put our bags on the bed. "I'm going into the city to meet up with Greg—you remember Mr. Miller—and a couple of other associates."

"Do you miss working in New York, Dad? Are you thinking of going back?" I ask him as I finish texting Seth to let him know I'm in Scarborough.

"Well, a couple of guys are talking about starting up a hedge fund. I could work out of Virginia most of the time and come up here once a week or so. I know your mother is tired of moving, and you have a good thing going with the wrestling team. We'll see what happens."

"You don't like working for the government?" I ask, although I already know the answer. During most of the drive up here, Dad had on Rush Limbaugh, and nothing gets Dad going like politics.

"You see, Benjamin," he says as he turns down the radio while there is a commercial break, "our country is going down a dangerous path. Big government leads toward totalitarianism. You know what that is, right?" He answered his own question. "That's someone telling you what to do and how to think."

"You mean like how you are with me?" I tease him. He punches me in the arm. "Hey, watch out! You're driving!"

"I thought I could make a difference working within the system," he goes on. "What a bunch of drones I work with." He shakes his head and then turns up the volume on the radio.

But tonight, we forget politics and work. Dad and I go out to eat at the Outback. It's nice because we get a seat near the bar and the TVs showing the various baseball games. I like talking sports with my father. He's more of a football fan than a baseball fan, but when it comes to sports, it really doesn't matter that much.

We talk about how wrestling is coming along for me. He asks me about other wrestlers on the team and who my competition is.

"You keep working out, Benjamin," he advises, "and you could be a good college wrestler. Don't underestimate yourself."

"Thanks, Dad," I say, although I'm thinking about another sport: girls. Girls and dating. If Brian is a lifeguard, surely he has access to meeting a lot of girls. Lifeguards are babe magnets.

Chapter 7

Dad and I get up a little after nine and get the free breakfast at the hotel before I drop him off at the train station to go up to New York. I text Brian and Seth. Brian texts back that he has stuff to do before he has lifeguard duty. Seth tells me to come over anytime.

"Have a good time," Dad tells me as I pull into the long parking lot that is mostly empty since it's a Saturday. "Be sure to check your phone messages. I'm not sure when I'll need you to pick me up."

"Sure, Dad." I'm feeling pretty good having the SUV all to myself for a day. "You have a good time too."

"Yeah, we will. We'll catch up on old times. I wish your mother came. We could have made it a night on the town." He genuinely looks bothered that she didn't come. "But who would look after Johnny? Or Rosie?"

He climbs out of the Tahoe and repeats his previous instructions to watch my phone for messages. Then I head out to Seth's house. Brian and Seth live in the same neighborhood, that old part of Scarborough where the houses are more spread out and look like they've been there for decades. There's a big oak tree in Seth's front yard where they still have a rope swing hanging from a massive limb.

I park along the curb. Seth greets me at the door.

"Hi ya, Benny!" He looks out at the Tahoe on the curb, with no parent inside. "Wow, you got wheels? Nice!"

"Yeah, I've been driving for a while," I tell him proudly. That's one good thing about Virginia: you can get your driver's license sooner than you can in New Jersey.

"No one's home," Seth tells me as we go through the hallway leading into the kitchen and den off to the side. "Dad and Mom went shopping."

"What's up with Brian?" I ask him after we've settled down in front of his television. "It's like he never wants to talk to me or anything. Is it something I said?"

I can ask Seth almost anything. He is one of the few people (maybe the only one) with whom I can let my guard down if something is bothering me.

He just shakes his head. "Brian's been that way forever, Benny. But lately, he's been in his own world. My mom says he has this 'little boy lost' look. She says Brian isn't comfortable in his skin yet. Like he looks like a man but still thinks like a boy. 'His emotions have not developed equally with his body,' she says, so he's all confused about stuff. You know my mother, all that psychoanalyzing!"

"It must be nice having a mother who can do that," I tell him. Seth's mother is a psychologist.

"Yeah, I guess," he says dismissively. "It gets on my nerves sometimes. But I talked to him last night, and he said we could go over to the pool, hang out there for a while, keep him company provided we don't talk to him too much!" Seth looks at me, smiling and shaking his head at the same time. "That's Brian for ya!"

I notice Seth has a tan and a nice friendly smile. My wingman could give me some competition if he wanted to.

When Seth and I get to the community pool, I spot Brian at the lifeguard chair before he sees us. I have to look at him for a minute to make sure this is the same kid I knew back when I lived here. I mean, this guy at the lifeguard station is different. He's not the same kid even from a year ago. Brian had a growth spurt, and he looks good.

"Brian sure has grown," I say to Seth, trying to sound objective but feeling a wave of jealousy. No round head for him—just high cheekbones and a perfect jawline, not too square, just strong enough to be called distinguished. And he has those eyes, deep set, like Johnny's soulful eyes. I can't believe my eyes.

"Yeah, what did I tell ya?" he says as he throws his towel on a lounge chair. I'm still taking in Brian's transformation when Seth says, "Well, let's say a quick hello and then take a dip."

"Oh, uh, hi," Brian says to us before he starts looking off at the swimmers. "How are ya, Benny?"

"I'm doing great, Brian. It's good to see you."

"Yeah, me too." He nods his head awkwardly, as if he's meeting with strangers.

"Well, uh, we'll have to catch up after I'm off."

"Yeah, that's the plan." I'm a little irritated by now, but Seth just shrugs it off and jumps in the pool. So I jump in to get cooled off and then survey the area.

Besides all the mothers and some fathers with little kids, there are girls who look to be around our age. I spot these two girls who look a little familiar, maybe from middle school or somewhere. Their faces look familiar, but the bodies, well, I try my best not to gawk. It's hard not to stare at girls when their bikinis show off perfectly smooth bronzed skin, long legs, not too curvy hips, small waists, and the pièce de résistance: perfectly formed breasts. Not too big, not too little.

Wow, they look real! I'm thinking. Not that I have much experience telling the difference between real bodies and surgically enhanced ones.

They look toward Brian and walk up to him. I would characterize the walk as seductive, but then it could just be their natural walk, like the way two gazelles gracefully walk through a field. But the look they're giving Brian is easily detectable to anyone. Anyone except Brian.

Brian tenses up. I can see even from in the pool that he's looking uncomfortable. *Is he nuts?* I'm thinking. *What's wrong with him? At least give them that goofy third grader grin.* So I'm seeing an opportunity. It is on me to break the ice.

"Hi," I hear the one in the yellow bikini say as she stands in front of him. "Don't I know you?"

Brian moves his head around her so he can still watch the pool. She graciously steps aside to his side. The other girl in the blue-and-white bikini has already placed herself to his left.

"Uh, I'm not sure," he mumbles.

"Hi!" I come onto the scene, injecting some enthusiasm. "I'm an old friend of Brian's—"

"Brian!" the girl in the yellow bikini says, as though a lightbulb goes on in her head. "That's it! I was in your American history class! Ninth grade? I'm Stacey."

"Oh, yeah." Brian nods vaguely and then looks out at the pool.

"I'm Ben," I tell them, using the adult version of my name. "I used to live here, but now I live in Virginia."

"Benny, I'm working here!" Brian objects. "I can't have people congregating around me."

"I'm *working* too," I lean over and whisper into his ear. Then I stand up and ask the girls if they would like a soda or water and if they want to hang out with Seth and me.

"We're just hanging out here until Brian's shift is over at five."

"Sure," Stacey says, and we go over to my duffel bag and I pull out some change for the drink machine. I motion Seth to get out of the pool to join us.

The girls—the other one's name is Laurie—Seth, and I sit around their table with an opened umbrella to shade us. At first, it's just small talk about school and what's been going on in Scarborough since I left. They seem like really nice girls, and I tell them that the three of us—Brian, Seth, and I—will be going out to the Eastside Mall and possibly a movie.

"Would you both like to join us?" I ask, and they say sure. Great. The evening is all set, so I tell Brian about our plans. I can't believe what he says next.

"Why did you invite them?" he asks me in an irritated voice, the kind a kid uses when his mother makes him turn off the TV so he can chat with relatives who came into town. "I didn't really remember that girl. I was just trying to be nice. Besides, it was supposed to be just us—you, me, and Seth—hanging out, maybe going to a movie."

"Brian"—I look at him, flabbergasted—"did you not see those girls? How could I let an opportunity like that get away?"

"You're girl crazy, Benny!" He looks at me, totally clueless.

"Brian," I say, trying to be patient, "I've just brought you a steak dinner! A five-course meal at a five-star restaurant, and this is how you repay me?"

"I just want to get a burger and fries." And he means it literally.

I'll make this short because I really can't stand reliving the humiliation. We all get to the mall. We get there thanks to my having a car and a license. The girls meet us at the food court. Then something happens between Stacey and Brian as we're eating our Chick-fil-As.

Stacey reaches across the table, touches Brian's hand, and looks at him with inviting eyes all the while chewing her sandwich. She's summoning him out of his boyish mind into the world of girls and sex. Something is happening in Brian's brain, like the pituitary gland (or whatever part of his brain has been on hold for all these years) starts revving up. It is broadcasting all over his dumb face. "It's okay, Brian. Girls are good."

"I love to go to Six Flags." She looks at him as she sips her Diet Coke.

"Me too." He looks at her, elbows on the edge of the table. A chicken finger dangles from his fingers on his right hand, dangerously close to falling on the waffle fries below.

"Then we should go!" She smiles.

"Okay," he tells her. And that is all she wrote, as they say. No playful bantering, no witty repartee for Brian. But then, Brian's not a roundhead. He has just waited to grow up into a good-looking guy and lets the girls come to him.

Meanwhile, Seth is still making small talk with Laurie. It's like this: Brian hits a home run, Seth gets on first, and I strike out.

Dad comes to my rescue when he calls me to let me know he'll be at the train station in half an hour. So I take the boys back home after Brian and Stacey exchange phone numbers and a passionate kiss that the rest of us weren't supposed to see, only I see it through the rearview mirror. I can't wait to get out of there.

It isn't until the next day after we pick up Elizabeth from Anna's house that Dad finds out about the details of my night on the town with my friends. Thanks to Elizabeth.

"Anna and I saw Benjamin and his friends with some girls at the food court," she tells Dad, as though she got a big news scoop. "Brian looked like he was in love with one of them!"

"Thanks, Elizabeth, for spying on us!"

"I wasn't spying," she protests. "We just happened to be there too."

Dad laughs. "Maybe you should have taken some pictures, Elizabeth! Maybe you should get a job at TMZ!"

"Maybe she should mind her own business." I'm just irritated now.

"Come on, Benjamin." Dad gives me a questioning look before returning his eyes to the road. "Where's your sense of humor?"

When we get home, Mom asks everyone about the trip. Dad and Elizabeth give positive reports. I tell her it was okay as I quickly pack up for wrestling camp.

"Just okay?" she asks. "All that time and expense your father put out and it was just okay? You could have gotten okay working for Mr. Lopez."

She never lets up. But then she reminds me, "Well, not much opportunity to get work now. After your wrestling camp, we have the week at the beach to go to."

That's right. The beach. Hope springs eternal.

Chapter 8

There's no summer camp devoted to the art of picking up girls. Except for the beach.

Visiting my mother's family in Myrtle Beach gives me lots of opportunities to meet girls, although it would be easier if I had my cousin Mark to act as my wingman. But Mark is such a Goody Two-shoes. His idea of fun at the beach is spending a half hour on the beach and the rest inside the condo, playing Risk with the other cousins. I mean I like Risk, the game. But I like taking risks at the beach too.

We are standing on the balcony of our fourth-floor condo, surveying the scene in front of us. Looks-wise, Mark is okay. I can imagine a girl wanting to get to know him. He's a personable guy. But when it comes to girls, Mark is another Brian. I mean, pre-Stacey Brian.

"Look at those girls over there." I point out a bevy of girls in bikinis parading by.

Mark looks at the same group with some consideration, looking to find something uniquely different about them.

"What about them?" He looks at me as though he's stumped.

"Aren't they good-looking?" I say, pointing out the obvious. *What is wrong with him?*

"I don't look at girls that way." Mark looks at me with his eyebrows arched.

"What do you mean by that?" I raise my voice a little too loudly.

Then my cousin says to me in a chiding way, "I don't look at girls like they are objects. Girls are people too."

"Of course they are people, Mark," I retort. "I like to get to know people. I guess you don't!"

"Gawking at girls is not the way to get to know them, Benjamin," he says in a really bratty manner. At least that's the way it comes out to me.

"Well, excuse me!" is all I can come up with. "What's your method then?"

Mark curls the left side of his upper lip. "What do you mean, 'what's my method?' Method for what?"

"Finding girls?"

"You're girl crazy." Mark shakes his head and walks back into the condo as Dad opens the sliding door to step out onto the terrace.

"Hi, Mark," Dad says as they sidestep one another. "What's going on?"

"Hi, Uncle Keith," Mark says as he steps back inside. "I'm going to check out what everyone's doing, maybe get up a game of Risk."

Dad stands next to me with his forearms resting on the rail. "Nice to be at the beach, isn't it?"

"Yeah," I answer without much enthusiasm. Mark's comments are still buzzing around in my head, putting a damper on the scene before me. So I think I can unload on Dad a little. He'd understand.

"I saw these really nice-looking girls, and I pointed them out to Mark, and he says, in this really snide way, 'I don't look at girls that way!' What a dork!" I shake my head.

"Aw, that's nice that Mark is being a gentleman!" Dad says with sincere admiration.

"So, what am I, a jerk?" I ask, annoyed that my own father doesn't take up for me.

"Oh, Benjamin, lighten up," Dad tells me. He's been doing that a lot lately, telling me to lighten up. Except when it comes to wrestling practice. Then it's "You've got to put more effort into your wrestling if you want to get anything out of it, Benjamin! Like scholarship money."

We continue to look out at the Atlantic Ocean and the wide beach below us. Then Dad slips in a lecture about being more involved with the family.

"You know, Benjamin, it would be nice if you'd spend more time with your cousins and less time trying to pick up girls," he says in gentle way, like he's trying not to offend me.

"I just want to have my own fun, Dad." I shift my weight from one foot to the other. I know what he means, to be honest. I don't spend much time with Grandpa, Grandma and my aunts and uncles. At least I am able to realize how antisocial I can be. Maybe it's crowds I don't like, I don't know. But that's not what is bothering me at the moment.

"I just wish I didn't have such a hard time with girls," I confess. "Maybe I am trying too hard."

Dad puts his arm around me. "When I was your age, I didn't go out much. I was too busy working and going to school. Plus, I didn't have a car to use …"

I've heard all about Dad's childhood before, so I start to drown him out in my head by focusing on the waves and the relaxing sound they make.

"…but you know, Benjamin"—Dad nudges my shoulder with the back of his hand, his way of indicating it's time for me to pay attention—"I remember when Johnny was a baby and your mother had to go out of town on business. You know, she went back to work after he was born …" The tone in his voice starts lightening up, and he smiles at the memory.

"I was at the park walking Johnny in his stroller, and these really attractive women came up to me and told me what an adorable baby I had. And I swear they were looking at *me* like they were flirting with me!"

"Really?" I'm partly smiling and wincing at the idea of attractive women flirting with my father. "Why would they be flirting with you?"

Dad shifts his legs back a little and puts more weight on his forearms resting on the rails. With his shoulders all hunched in, he gives me this pointer: "You know, Benjamin, women seem to like to see men holding babies! It's weird, huh? But babies are a babe magnet!"

"How's that?" I ask skeptically.

"I think when a woman sees you with a baby, she's thinking you have a nurturing side, a caring side. She figures you'll be that way with her too."

"Oh." I nod.

"Of course, I was already married, so it was a moot point for me." Dad presses his lips and nods. "But you—you could borrow your cousin Heather's baby for a while, take her out to the beach, see what happens, ha-ha!"

"Yeah, right, Dad." I shake my head at the very thought of his suggestion.

"You could even use a line like 'Won't you be my baby?'"

"You're joking, right?" I wrinkle my nose. Sometimes it's hard to tell if Dad's ribbing me or being serious. My father has given me a series of stupid pickup lines to try out: "Did it hurt when you fell down from heaven?" "You must be wearing space pants because your body is out of this world!" "You look like a library book I want to check out!" I wonder how he ever got Mom to marry him. He gives me a gentle punch in the arm and turns to leave.

Babies have never been my strong suit. The youngest kids I ever babysat were boys, ages seven and nine. They're fun at that age. Heather is Mark's older sister by ten years. She's already married and has Caitlin, who is one and a half, and Heather announced at dinner the night before that she and Tim were going to have another one.

Dad's remarks about spending more time with the family echo Mom's. She is always griping that I don't spend enough time with the extended family. "You're always going off, trying to meet other people," she gripes, "as though you're embarrassed to be around your family!" In a sense she's right.

So Dad's idea would kill two birds with one stone, I'm thinking. *Spend some time with the family plus get girls.* The whole idea seems strange, like on those cooking shows Mom and Elizabeth watch on occasion, where they put together a dish that has ingredients that don't go together, like bacon on top of ice cream or something. But I'm thinking it just might work, so I offer my services to my cousin Heather for the night.

"Benjamin, that's so nice of you to want to look after Caitlin!" My cousin Heather looks at me so appreciatively, I almost feel guilty taking her kid.

"Oh, my pleasure, Heather." I smile at her with as much sincerity as I can muster. "I figure I need some practice with kids anyway. You and Tim go ahead and have some adult time together."

"Well, be careful," Mom calls out from the galley kitchen. "Don't let her get too close to the waves. And don't let her out of your sight!"

"Of course, Mom," I say. "Don't you think I know anything about kids?"

"Well—"

But before she can say anything, I volunteer to look after Johnny, as well, as a way of getting her to put a lid on any doubts regarding my babysitting abilities. "Johnny can go to the beach with Caitlin and me."

"Oh, that would be nice." Mom is all placated now. "Thanks. I'm going to go get Rosie from the kennel and bring her out to the beach." Dogs are allowed to go on the beach in the mornings before nine and after five o'clock in the evening. Those are Mom's favorite times on the beach.

Fortunately, Caitlin is a good baby, the kind that seems happy all the time, unlike some of my younger cousins, who are what my mother calls fussbudgets. (I will refrain from stating their names. After all, they can't help it.) She readily takes my hand, and we head to the elevator to go out to the beach.

Lo and behold, little Caitlin, Johnny, and I run into Cousin Mark, who is stepping out of the elevator as we are getting on.

"Where are you going?" he asks me, still in the elevator as I get on. He steps out but keeps his hand over the elevator door. He gives me a suspicious look, which gets me irritated.

"I'm going to the beach." I state the obvious as I hold Caitlin's hand. "Is that okay?"

"Why are you taking Caitlin?" He looks at me as though I have an ulterior motive. *Well, I guess I do,* I admit to myself, *but what's that to him?*

"I'm babysitting for Heather and Tim!"

"Oh." He looks perplexed and then says, "I'll help you out," and steps back into the elevator. For me to object would look really suspicious, not to mention standoffish. To be honest, I could use the help, and it would be good to pass little Caitlin off to Mark when (I'm not even thinking if at this point) I meet up with a girl. Still, I resent his butting in.

The four of us walk the wooden pathway that leads to the beach. As I get to the steps leading down to the sand, I see my mission right before me: two long-legged, pretty girls with their long amber-colored hair pulled back into ponytails, playing beach volleyball in bikinis. One of the girls is taller than the other by several inches. She looks to be the one in control, like a coach. "That was a great shot!" she tells the other girl, who's not bad in terms of looks and athleticism, but not as good as the taller girl. I figure I could win with either one.

Johnny runs over to the waves, thankfully. That's his thing, running along in the shallow waves, making his weird noises, as though he is competing with the roar of the ocean. He starts up with this song, "Take On Me." It's one of those techno songs from the eighties. Johnny has a whole bunch of them stashed away in his head, along with his Beatles repertoire. It keeps him entertained, and at any rate, at least he's out of the way.

I figure this is my moment to make an impression with the volleyball girls, so I pick up Caitlin. Naturally I'm not as well practiced at it as Mark.

"That's not how you're supposed to hold a baby, Benjamin," he admonishes me like my mother. "You're holding her like an infant. She's a big girl. Hold her on your hip. Like this."

"I'm fine," I snap as I twist the little kid around into an upright position. She's giggling. "See?" I give Mark a look of triumph.

Then a volleyball lands right on my head and rolls onto Caitlin's. A look of confusion comes over her face, as if she doesn't know whether to shrug it off or cry. Mark gets all freaked out, and then she starts wailing.

"Give her to me!" He grabs her. The girls come running over, saying, "Oh my God!" over and over.

"Are y'all okay?" the taller one asks. "Poor thing, I'm so sorry!"

Caitlin, bless her heart, goes from wailing to softly heaving in seconds. "Oh, she's okay," I try to assure the girls. "See?" Caitlin starts squirming and holds out her arms to Mark, who takes her.

"You're okay, Caitlin." Mark smiles at her and tickles her belly, and she starts laughing.

"What a cute little girl!" the taller one tells us. We later learn her name is Christy. My impression of girls named Christy (which comes from the stadium seats, where my eyes tend to fall on head cheerleader Christy Forester) is that they are fireballs. This Christy is no exception. She is the captain of her school's volleyball team ("Volleyball is in my blood!" she explains). Christy talks in exclamation points.

"It's great that y'all are watching after your little cousin!" she tells us after we've been talking for a while. We learn that she and Maddie are staying with Christy's family at the same condo building we are in.

"Well, she's actually my niece," Mark corrects her.

"Wow! You're an uncle already? That's neat," Maddie sneaks in a comment. She seems nice but doesn't say much after that. She lets Christy do all the talking.

Then Johnny, who's been running in circles in the waves this whole time, shrieks out a line from the song: "I'll be gooooooone! Oh, oh, oh, OH!"

"Oh my God! Is that guy okay?" Christy asks.

"Yeah, he's my brother," I answer, a little embarrassed. "He does that. He has autism."

"Wow! I have a neighbor who has a kid like that!" Christy says. "I don't know him, but I see him walking around every once in a while. Don't you think you ought to go and see if he's okay?"

"No, he's fine," I insist as Johnny stays stuck on the "I'll be gooooooone!" line. Christy looks unsure.

"Well, I guess you should know, you're his brother." She shrugs but still gives me a look that says I ought to feel guilty about leaving Johnny out. But then she switches gears and turns her attention to Mark, holding Caitlin.

"Hey, Mark." She gives him a gentle punch in the arm. "Why don't we all take a walk with little Caitlin?"

"Well"—Mark suddenly looks intently at the sand—"I guess so. But"—then he delivers this cheesy line, "can you put on a cover-up?"

Christy's jaw drops, and then she yells, "Mark, you are the bomb! The bomb!" She gives him a big smile. "I've never had a guy tell me that! Most guys want me for one thing, my athletic prowess! Ha-ha! You are such a gentleman, Mark!"

She gives him a playful nudge on the arm and leads the five of us northward. I'm with Maddie, following behind Mark, Caitlin, and Christy. Unfortunately, Maddie is as quiet as Christy is talkative. I just want to leave.

"I should probably go back and look after my brother," I say as we walk past the next condo building over. Talk about feeling awkward. Talking to Maddie is like pulling teeth. And I really need to get away.

Later, Christy asks Mark to go to the Pavilion with her the next night. She asks him to tell me to accompany Maddie, which I do.

My parents are thrilled to see me going out on a double date.

"Hey, Benjamin, I was only half kidding about the baby thing," Dad says, grinning ear to ear, "but I guess it worked!"

"See what happens when you stick with yoah family?" says Rosie, via Mom. *"Ah love spending time with mah family!"*

"We love you too, Rosie, but it's time to go back to the kennel." Mom gives her a pat.

So I guess, maybe technically, I've had my first date. Maddie wouldn't have been so bad if she didn't keep her arms crossed the whole time. She wasn't mean or hostile or anything—just uncomfortable-looking. Christy pulled me aside and told me Maddie just broke up with her boyfriend, so "she's still feeling it, you know."

So it turned out that Dad's baby trick worked really well—for Mark. But then Mark is such a pushover. Christy looked at Mark as a dog who could easily be trained, and boy, was she right. Well, I'm not a dog, and I definitely don't need a girl like Christy. But still, Mark got credited for getting me a date.

What's wrong with me? Is this as good as it gets for me? Or maybe a better question is, what is wrong with guys like Brian and Mark, ready to let a girl lead them by the nose? Where's a girl for me? Maybe I'm coming off as too desperate. Maybe it's my round head. Maybe I smell bad and no one has the nerve to tell me.

My aunt Sarah, Mark's mother, finds me the next day on the sofa, looking forlorn. At least that's the way she says I look. Aunt

Sarah is really nice, but she's the kind of person who you have to watch your mouth with. Still, she means well.

"You know, Benjamin"—she looks at me with a smile—"your name means 'son of my right hand.'"

"Really?" I nod, trying to be polite.

"It's from the Bible," she continues. "Jacob gave that name to his second son. He changed it from Ben-omi, the name Rachel originally gave her son. Before she died."

"Oh." I nod and try to keep smiling.

"Ben-omi means 'my son is a real pain,'" Aunt Sarah explains.

"Oh, yeah." I let out a sad laugh. "I can be that. That's for sure."

"But you are quite a young man, Benjamin." She smiles at me gently, and all I can do is look away, as it's starting to get uncomfortable. "I know you are your parents' right-hand man. Never forget God has a plan for you."

"Thanks, Aunt Sarah." I nod politely. *It would be nice if God let me in on the plan,* I'm thinking. I know she means well, though I don't think about God a lot, to be honest. When I do, I just think about this old man up there playing tricks on me. I start thinking I'm ready for summer to be over. Summer's a great time if you have a girlfriend. If you don't, you may as well be in prison, spending all your time playing video games, watching TV, and reading. And doing a little wrestling.

Chapter 9

"Why do they have to stay in my room?"

Aunt Terry and Uncle Doug were coming into town. It's the second Saturday in August already, and they called to announce they still had time on their schedule to pay us a visit. Aunt Terry is my father's older sister, and her husband Doug is a retired professor. Their son lives in DC, so they said they'd stop by for a night or two.

"Because, Benjamin," Mom explains as she throws my clothes on my bedroom floor out into the hallway, expecting me to go fetch them and put them in the washer, "Johnny's bedroom has twin beds and Elizabeth's room looks too girly." She heaves a big sigh as she throws off the bedcover. "Besides, it's a good excuse to clean up your room!"

I help Mom get the sheets off the bed. I like Aunt Terry and Uncle Doug well enough, but they are a source of irritation to my father, who hates Terry's politics. "Whatever you do, don't talk about politics!" Mom tells me with exasperation.

"Tell that to Dad!" I laugh. Mom smiles back at me and shakes her head. What really irks my mother is that Aunt Terry tends to be somewhat of a moocher. She takes advantage of my father's penchant for being a little too generous with picking up the check every time we go out to eat. And we go out to eat every time they come to visit.

"It's always 'We'll get it next time!'" Mom mimics Aunt Terry's nasally Wisconsin accent. "But next time never comes!"

"She has T. rex arms!" Dad chimes in as he ascends the stairs and comes into my room. He holds his elbows right to his chest and holds up his hands in a clawlike fashion. "It's always 'I would get the check but I can't reach it!'"

Mom laughs at Dad's send-up of Aunt Terry and then sighs. "Yep, that's Terry all right. A big Ethel Merman voice and a tight wallet. But tonight, I'm fixing a roast for dinner and we can eat in the dining room. And, sweetheart, please don't bring up politics!"

"I won't," Dad says rather defensively. "But if she still has those bumper stickers on her car, she's going to have to park it on the street!"

"What bumper stickers?" I ask.

"They say 'Friends don't let friends vote Republican' and 'Well behaved women rarely make history'! Huh, tell that to Margaret Thatcher!"

"Okay, Dad, I know, I know." I just don't want him to start on a rant about politics, so I head toward the laundry room to start a load. To be honest, I think her T. rex arms bother him more and the political stuff is just a cover. Mom agrees. "Keith, we're going to stay away from politics and just talk about family things."

"I know that, Diane," Dad says defensively. "Remind Terry of that too, why don't you."

Actually, Aunt Terry and Uncle Doug are kind of fun. Aunt Terry is a singer and performs at hotel lounges and weddings. She even teaches a couple of classes where Uncle Doug taught. It's all the old music and show tunes. Not my kind of thing, but if it floats your boat, she's pretty good. She is very dramatic in the way she carries on conversations. She is a tall woman, with reddish hair and a big face, and she uses her face to great effect. She speaks as if everyone is an audience and she is a one-woman show.

The doorbell rings as I gather all my bedding to spend the night in the basement, which, to be honest, I don't mind so much, as I spend most of my nights down there anyway, playing games and watching television. I look down from the upstairs landing onto the two-story foyer. It's them.

"Hello, everybody! We made it!" she almost sings at the top of her voice as Dad opens up the front door. She gives him a hug and some air kisses on both cheeks as Mom comes into the foyer. Uncle Doug, who looks like an old hound dog, stands slightly behind her.

"Hello," he says perfunctorily.

"We've been driving all day today, just stopping for gas. So we don't want to sit right now. Just tell us where to put our luggage." She motions to Uncle Doug to pick up the bags, as if he were a bellhop.

Rosie bounces into the foyer, jumping up on Aunt Terry.

"Agh!" she screams and tries to make nice. "Hi, dog!"

"Rosie, come!" Mom grabs the dog by the collar and invites the guests into the kitchen.

"What a lovely house! Diane, you really fixed it up so nice—"

"Thank you," Mom manages to squeeze in.

"I love the colors! It's bigger than the house in New Jersey, which I loved too. Much better than our dinky little house in Madison! We've done some renovation. You know it's near the university. Benjamin! Little Ben-Ben!" She sees me descending the back set of stairs leading to the kitchen. "Come give your aunt Terry a hug!"

"Hi" is all I can say before getting squeezed to death. As a wrestler, I envy her strong arm.

I hear the side door from the garage opening. Elizabeth has just returned from a run in the neighborhood. By this time, we've all moved to the kitchen. Johnny, who all this time has been sitting in the sunroom on the sofa, sings some song I can't make out. Mom's getting glasses of water.

"Was that Elizabeth we saw running as we were driving through your neighborhood?"

"Hi, Aunt Terry," she says with heavier breath than normal. She's been into running lately, and she's gotten pretty good. "Hi, Uncle Doug."

"We didn't recognize you!" Terry says apologetically as she dashes to give her niece a hug. "You've grown so much in just a few years! And I was going to say that Benjamin looks so grown-up, as well."

Then she looks over the counter that separates the kitchen and the sunroom. "Johnny!" She smiles like a celebrity. "What are you singing?" She walks from the kitchen into the sunroom like she's a guest on a talk show, sits right next to him, and gives him a side hug. This causes Johnny to get up and start pacing and flapping his arms. But that doesn't deter her from performing.

"And here's to you, Mrs. Robinson, Jesus loves you more than you will know. Whoa, whoa, whoa!" Aunt Terry starts singing what Johnny was singing, making the lyrics clearer. She's totally oblivious to Johnny's anxiety.

"I love that song, Johnny! You know, I remember that song when it first came out." She chuckles. "I was real young, of course—much younger than you are now!"

"Right!" Dad laughs. "Can I get anyone anything? Something to drink?"

"We're good," Aunt Terry says. "Oh, what a lovely family room, Diane." She walks from the sunroom into the family, looking at the curtains. "I love these drapes!"

"Thanks," Mom says while attempting to calm Johnny down.

Aunt Terry and Uncle Doug take a seat on the love seat while Dad sits in his usual spot on the large sofa. I sit in the large armchair that no one usually sits in except when company is here. Elizabeth excuses herself to go take a shower. Mom and Johnny are still in the sunroom. He's flapping his arms frantically like a bird that can't take off because his wings have been clipped. If he doesn't settle down, he could have a meltdown.

"Use your words, Johnny," Mom coaxes him. "Use your words! What do you want?"

"I … want … *music!*" he says frantically. Mom gets his iPod, which is sitting on the side table next to the sofa, and unwraps the earphones.

"What music, Johnny?" Johnny looks at Mom desperately. "It's okay, Johnny. Use your words."

"Bea-tles!" Mom taps on the iPod to get to the Beatles. "What song, Johnny?"

"Mackwell Silber Hammer!" Johnny lets out a deep breath.

"Okay, 'Maxwell's Silver Hammer it is.'" Mom lets out a sigh of relief, as well. He goes back, sits on his sofa, and stares out the window. As long as Johnny gets what he wants, crises are avoided.

"Bang! Bang! Maxwell's silver hammer came down upon her head!" Aunt Terry sways as she sings. She can sing any old song there is. "I loved the Beatles when I was young." She smiles as she gives Uncle Doug a pat on the knee. She tells a story about them being on some show back in the sixties, and it was a big deal.

"I was babysitting you, Keith." She loves to tell anecdotes about their childhood. "One night, I put Keith in the tub. He was just three or four years old. Anyway, I told him I'd get him out as soon as the Beatles were finished playing."

"I was in the tub for over an hour!" Dad interjects. I don't know if he really remembers or the story has been told for so many years. But they get a laugh from it every time.

"By the time I got poor Keith out, he was just a little raisin!" Aunt Terry laughs heartily.

Then Dad leans over to Mom, flaps his eyebrows up and down like an old comedian, and talks out of the side of his mouth. "I hope *you* don't say that when you see me coming out of the tub!"

"Keith!" Mom slaps him playfully. I get up from the sofa and manage to slip out unnoticed.

Dinner in the dining room means a special occasion where Mom puts out the best dishes and place settings. I think Mom is doing it to impress Aunt Terry on her hosting and cooking skills. She insists on making a big deal of the visit. After all, Aunt Terry always compliments Mom on her decorating skills. Mom loves that.

We sit with Dad at the head and Mom at the opposite end. I sit next to Aunt Terry, with Uncle Doug on the other side, closer to Mom. Johnny and Elizabeth sit on the side closest to the kitchen.

"We will be going into DC tomorrow to see Robbie, our son," she announces after we all get our helpings of garlic mashed potatoes, asparagus, and roast. "You remember your cousin Rob?" She leaned over to me. "You saw him at your cousin Peter's wedding. Anyway, he's clerking for Chief Justice Sonia Sotomayor." Aunt Terry seems to relish the opportunity to name-drop."

"Oh" is all Dad says.

"Well, he's one of a bunch of lawyers who works there," Uncle Doug says, playing down the connection. "Not very senior. "I don't think he's actually even met her yet."

"Well, it's still a big deal." Aunt Terry digs her fork in the back of Uncle Doug's hand. "We're going to have lunch with him somewhere in Georgetown. He has a bachelor pad in the city"— she makes little quotation signs on the words "bachelor pad"—"so we don't want to intrude on him too much." She chuckles. "It's his time to live the big city life! You know, with his friends in high places!"

Dad manages to change the subject. "So, did you stop off and visit anyone since you left Wisconsin?"

"Mmm." Aunt Terry holds up her finger as she takes a swig of iced tea. "We saw Harry and stayed the night in Cincinnati. We had a great time!"

"We took in a baseball game," Uncle Doug adds.

"Yeah, Harry's a big Reds fan," Dad says. "How are he and Jessica?"

"They're doing fine," Aunt Terry says. "They're just getting ready for Anthony to start college. He's going to the University of Miami. In Ohio, not Florida!" She takes another bite of garlic mashed potatoes and then says, "It's so nice to see you and Diane, Keith! I'm so glad we have *normal* relatives to visit! Unlike you know who!"

"Who?" I manage to ask even though I can guess the answer: Aunt Monica, the black sheep of the family. She's the only sibling out of Dad's five that I've never met.

"Your Aunt Monica," Dad answers. "She's dead to the family."

"Except at funerals," Aunt Terry adds. "We allow her at funerals, as long as she doesn't talk."

"She wasn't at Mom's funeral," Dad says as he cuts into his roast.

"She was!" Aunt Terry says in a gossipy way. "She sat at the back of the church, weeping like she was the chief mourner! But she came late and left early."

"Ironic, isn't it? When in fact she killed Mom." Dad shakes his head. "Or at least broke her heart."

"That's too bad" is all I can say.

"How did she do that?" Inquiring minds like Elizabeth's want to know.

"It's a long story," Aunt Terry explains, taking a brief pause before her monologue. "Your aunt Monica was always a rebel, even when we were growing up. She was a real feminist back in the seventies. She was a real believer, didn't shave her legs or underarms for years!"

"It was three years," Uncle Doug adds. "She looked like a grizzly."

"Eew!" Elizabeth makes a face.

"That's right, Elizabeth—eeyooo!" Aunt Terry continues. "Then she had an abortion—"

"We don't need to go into that, Terry," Dad warns.

"Oh, we all had abortions back in the 1970s!" Aunt Terry waves him off with the back of her hand. "Not literally, but figuratively."

"How can you have a figurative abortion, Terry?" Dad asks.

"So anyway," she continues, "one day, she and Mother have this big argument about abortion." Aunt Terry's eyes dart around the table, demanding everyone's attention. "Well, Mother—may she rest in peace—said something about how bad abortion was, which set Monica off. 'How would you like it if I aborted you, Monica?' Mother asks her. Then Monica looks at our mother and says, 'Well, Mother, you were never a mother to me!'"

Aunt Terry's eyes land on me, putting me in the spotlight. She presses her lips until they disappear in her mouth. I try to think of something to say.

"That's too bad," I say feebly.

Aunt Terry heaves a big sigh and says, "Anyhoooo, let's talk about you, Benjamin! Look at you. You're such a big kid now. I remember when you were just a little boy with your thumb in your mouth and a blanket in one hand. Just like Linus!"

Now she is starting to really irritate me. I hate being patronized. She can talk about Dad being a shriveled-up raisin in the bathtub all she wants. But I'm not a little kid anymore, in case she hasn't noticed.

"With a big beautiful round head!" She laughs.

"He doesn't have a round head!" Mom says with a tight smile.

"Oh, he did!" Aunt Terry insists. "It was like a ball!"

"At least I don't have T. rex arms!" I blurt out. I can't help it. It just spills out, and both my parents glare at me with that "don't go there" look.

"What do you mean, 'T. rex arms'?" Aunt Terry smiles and then looks perplexed. "What's T. rex arms?"

"I'm not sure," Mom mumbles.

Then Elizabeth offers a visual by tucking up her elbows into her sides and holding up her hands like grasping claws and blurts out, laughing, "It means you can't pick up a check!"

Mom and Dad look mortified.

Well, welcome to my world, Mom and Dad! I'm thinking. *Enjoy the aftershocks of Elizabeth's big mouth.*

It's funny. When a dog shows his lower teeth, it means he's happy. But with Aunt Terry, who is now baring hers, it looks menacing. She turns her wrath on Dad.

"Are you implying that I'm cheap, Keith?" She is growling now, threatening to attack.

"I'm sure it doesn't mean anything, Terry," Uncle Doug says, leaning toward Aunt Terry.

"I'll handle this, Doug!" she snarls.

"Go to bathroom!" Johnny yells. "Go to *bathroom*!"

"Go to the bathroom, Johnny," Moms tells him. Johnny jumps out of his chair, runs to the bathroom in the hallway, and slams the door. Lucky Johnny. When he gets uncomfortable, he can blame his autism. The rest of us have to suffer the slings and arrows of an outrageous aunt.

"It's just a joke, Terry," Dad says matter-of-factly. "Everyone jokes about how *thrifty* you are. Besides, I don't mind paying for dinners."

"Keith, Terry's paid for things," Mom says weakly.

"Don't forget about the time we took *your* family out to that all-you- can-eat seafood buffet!" She jabs her fork toward Dad.

Touché, Aunt Terry.

"You got a couple of 'buy one entrée, get one free' coupons." Dad shrugs. "Plus, kids ate free!"

"Kids under *five ate free*!" Aunt Terry is trying her best to sound as blasé as Dad, but her skills as an actress are failing her. "Elizabeth told the hostess she was six"—Aunt Terry turns to Elizabeth and holds up her hands to her shoulders—"and I admire you for your honesty, Elizabeth." She realizes she just made the T. rex pose and smiles as she extends her arms out toward Elizabeth.

"Really, it's okay, Terry!" Dad says as he reaches for his glass of iced tea.

"Well." Aunt Terry heaves a big sigh, dabs her mouth with her napkin, and pushes herself from the table. "I'm going. Come on, Doug. Thank you for dinner, Diane."

Mom smiles meekly. Aunt Terry and Uncle Doug head upstairs. Mom, Dad, Elizabeth, and I sit like we're all deer in the headlights.

"Let's go watch the game, Benjamin," Dad says after a moment and gets up from the table. "That was a good dinner, Diane. Thank you."

"I'm glad you liked it," Mom answers, as if nothing happened.

After the game, I'm bringing up my blanket and pillow, naturally assuming Aunt Terry and Uncle Doug had left.

"Why are you bringing your blanket up? I thought you wanted to sleep in the basement," Mom says as I get to the top of the stairs.

"Aunt Terry said they were going," I say, starting to get annoyed.

"She meant they were going upstairs to your room," Mom says. "You didn't expect that she would pay for a hotel room … in DC!" She laughs. "That's over a hundred dollars a night!"

"What about staying with cousin Rob?"

"I'm sure his place is too small, or maybe he has roommates. Either way, Aunt Terry and Uncle Doug are staying for a couple of days."

"But Dad insulted her! He accused her of having T. rex arms. If someone insulted me like that, I'd leave."

"Really? And where would you go, and how would you pay for it?" I don't want to go there with Mom. Why does she always bring up money with me? She's always comparing me to how frugal Elizabeth is with her allowance money.

"Why do we put up with relatives?" I sigh.

"Because they're family, Benjamin," Mom says. "Now, just don't let her remarks get to you. She didn't mean anything by it."

"Do I still have a round head, Mom?" I ask her.

"No!" She rolls her eyes, exasperated at having to answer a question I've asked her more than once. She looks over at the dog, who is right behind her.

"Well," she channels Rosie, *"Ah think it is bettuh to have a round he-ad than have T. rex ahrms!"*

Nuggets of wisdom from the family dog. *Thanks, Mom. I'll keep that in mind this school year.*

The rest of Aunt Terry and Uncle Doug's visit goes by as though nothing was ever said. Everybody is very polite to each other. Dad offers to drive them to DC and show them around. I don't have anything else to do, so I go along with the rest of the family. Dad suggests we go out to lunch at this nice restaurant he knows.

"Lunch?" Aunt Terry asks. "I don't know. Doug and I—"

"Oh, come on, it's our treat," Dad says. Mom has a funny look on her face, and I don't mean ha-ha funny.

"Well," Aunt Terry drawls and then says quickly, "okay, but next time we'll pick up the check."

And so it goes, like nothing ever happened. In fact, that's how this summer has gone. Like nothing ever happened.

Chapter 10

I hadn't spoken to Brian or Seth since that night I got them some girls. And I have to admit I felt relieved when Seth Skyped me a few days after Aunt Terry left and told me nothing ever came of that girl he paired up with. I had my friend back.

"Jeez, Benny, I got rid of her as fast as I could!" He looks as if he escaped from a haunted house or something. "She was like a stalker, sending me text messages ten times a day and even calling me at home!"

"That's a little weird," I say.

"You bet it is! I just blanked her out."

"So how is Brian and Stacey?" I am hoping for more good news—that is, that they aren't together. I know that sounds mean, but I can't help it.

"They still go out, but you know Brian. This can only last for so long."

"What do you mean?"

"Oh, come on, Benny!" Seth laughs. "This is Brian we're talking about. The guy who couldn't stay at your house overnight because he couldn't take a number two in anyone else's house!"

"Yeah, that's true." I shake my head. "He'd always say, 'That's a little personal!'"

"So I dunno about him," Seth says, "but then, I haven't seen him for a couple of weeks. It's like he's dropped off the planet. But

I can't afford to get involved with someone. I've got to concentrate on getting into Rutgers and getting my GPA up and the SATs."

"Seth, there's other things to think about," I counter. "Life's not just grades and SAT scores."

"So what are you doing this year, Benny?"

It is a loaded question even though he didn't mean it to be. What do I want? Besides a girl? Besides respect?

"Well, you gotta have fun," I say lamely. "What do you do for fun?"

"Watch the play-offs! Who do you see going into the World Series?"

So we go off on baseball. It's okay, though. Thank God for sports. It gives us hours of conversation. But I miss Seth. I miss having someone to sit at lunch with like we did in middle school. He really came through for me then.

There was this kid Jason, who was in three of my classes back in sixth grade. His eighth grade sister was a junior camp counselor at the camp I went to before going into seventh grade. She was blonde and hot, especially at the camp dance night. Jason didn't want me, a mere sixth grader, making any moves on her.

"Dude, you're not good enough for her," he told me.

"I beg to differ," I taunted, and just to up the ante, I said, "I bet I'm just her type." I couldn't believe what I had just said. *What am I doing? Just fake it, Ben,* I told myself.

"Hi, Kristin," I said, trying to keep my voice low and steady. I buried my chin into my chest to keep it from shaking.

"Hello, Benny!" She smiled and patted me on the shoulder. Kristen was a few inches taller than me. She could have been a model.

"It's a nice dance, isn't it?"

"Well," she said, still smiling, "yeah, it's nice." After a brief pause, she added, "Not much dancing going on."

"Well, we'll have to change that, won't we?" I looked straight at her, and she laughed.

"Okay, Benny, why not?" It was not exactly a resounding yes, but I figured I'd take it.

The DJ played "Let's Get It Started." She loved that song, she said. I admit, I'm not the greatest dancer, but I didn't care. I got Jason's sister on the dance floor. I couldn't stop smiling … and giving him the occasional look of triumph.

He kept glaring at me, and after the song he walked over to me and said, "Dude, don't go any further with my sister."

"Why, Jase? I found a girl. Now go get one for yourself and quit worrying about me." I wasn't about to give up my newfound confidence.

Then they played that James Blunt song "You're Beautiful." I wasn't about to let this opportunity pass me by.

Feel the fear and do it anyway, I kept telling myself.

"Would you like to dance one more time?" I think she heard the quiver in my voice. I gave her the puppy dog eyes.

"Sure." She tousled my hair and took pity on me. Kristen looked at me with a closed-mouth smile that said, "Aw, aren't you a cute little pup." But I didn't care. I got to the next level.

I held her close but not too tight. I wanted to show her I respected her. Plus, I wasn't sure if my breath was okay. I mean, I didn't think I would have to check my breath. I never had to before. So I turned my head the opposite way. And there was Jason, just shaking his head at me. I just smiled. I was in the big leagues now. I had in my arms an older woman. It felt good. Not to be crude or anything, but I still feel a tingle up my leg, if you know what I mean.

When the camp bus took us back to the parking lot of the grocery store, Mom was waiting in the car with Rosie in tow. Stepping off the bus and walking to the car was like walking on clouds. Okay, that's a cliché, I know, but it's a cliché because it's true. That's what love must feel like.

"Well, look at that smile on your face!" Mom remarked as I strapped on my seat belt. "You must have had a pretty good time."

"Yeah, I'd say it was a pretty good time," I said, beaming.

"Mah human puppy Benjahmin is a real pahtay boy," "Rosie" said.

"Dude, my sister's a lesbian, and it's all your fault," Jason told me in the hallway between classes. So went my first day of seventh grade.

"What!" Was Jason saying this to try to cool my passions for his sister, or could it be true?

"That's right," said his friend standing next to him. "Kristen's gay, so lay off. She doesn't want your kind."

"What do you mean, *my* kind? Don't you mean *our* kind?" I asked as I pointed to each of us *boys*. "And by the way, Jason, I didn't turn your sister gay. She was born that way."

"I know that, idiot." He sneered at me.

"Then don't say it's my fault," I said with finality. Then I just walked off to class.

But I couldn't help but think that maybe Jason was right; I turned his sister gay or at least tipped her over the edge. All through science class I kept thinking, *What did I do? What did I say? Was it the way I smelled? Maybe I was releasing too many male hormones at the time, and it proved too much for her fragile system.* I read somewhere that the female system (or whatever you want to call it) is fickle, like it could go either way, gay or straight, at a very crucial point in its development.

I sought some kind of solace from Seth during lunch.

"Don't blame yourself, Ben," Seth said with compassion coming out of every syllable. He's good at that kind of thing, sounding sympathetic. He got it from his psychologist mother.

"But she's so good-looking," I said, dumbfounded.

"Ben, not all lesbians are ugly," Seth informed me as he took a bite out of his peanut butter and jelly sandwich. "That is an ugly stereotype. Many lesbians are quite attractive." Seth spoke with such authority. Maybe he really had read all of those psychology books his mother had on their basement bookshelves. I really wanted to believe him, even though in the back of my mind, I knew Seth was just as lost about girls as I was.

"The important thing for you to know is, you did not cause Jason's sister to become a lesbian. Not that there is anything wrong with being a lesbian."

The bell rang, and I thanked Seth for his insights as we got up and cleared the trash off the table.

"Don't worry, Ben. There are other fish in the sea," Seth said as he left to go to his class. "And not all of them are lesbians."

"I'll remember to avoid fishing in the lesbian sea," I said.

"Ben! I think that's homophobic," he chided me.

"Sorry, didn't mean to be." I headed off to class.

I sure could use a friend like Seth, one who lives in Adele. But I haven't found one yet.

chapter 11

I get my class schedule before I head to the school gym to work out with the wrestling team for one final workout before the school year starts. I've got a precalculus class first thing, which is going to be hard for me since the mornings are not my best time. But I'm determined to make this year a positive one. I'm going to try to be upbeat and make friends.

I try this new approach in wrestling practice. I even try with Blake.

"So, Blake, are you ready for your senior year?" I ask, trying to start a conversation.

"Shut up, douche bag," he says, wiping his face with his towel. I decide not to let this bother me. Blake is hopeless, and it would be a waste of time to try to be nice to him. Still, I'm not going to give up.

North Central High is kind of shaped like an H. It is made up of two big two-story buildings connected by the main part that has all the administrative offices. The cafeteria, gym, and theater are all on one side. My precalculus class is on the second floor on the other side, close to the front of the school.

I've never had a class in this section. I've always associated it with Johnny, because his autism class is on the corner. I've only been in his classroom once or twice with Mom, when they had a Christmas (or rather winter holiday, to be politically correct) party, and that was only for a few minutes. Technically, Johnny "graduates" this year because this is his senior year. But schools are required to keep kids like him on until they are twenty-one. But Mom and his teacher are making a big deal about this being his senior year—as if he is going to get senioritis or something! As if this is the year he will go to the prom!

I like to sit near the door in just about any class I'm in, save history. It always makes for an easy exit. Then I think, *No, this year, I'm going to mix in more with people, try to be more open.* So I get into class, and I'm the third kid to come in. I decide to sit in the second desk in the third row. Then a whole slew of kids come in. One of them is Blake. He doesn't see me stare at him as he passes my row and heads straight for the row near the window. I'm a little jolted.

Blake's an idiot, I'm thinking. *How did he get into precalculus? Well, he is a senior this year. He should be in calculus if he's serious about going to any good school for college. And what's a senior doing in a math class anyway? Shouldn't he have all easy classes for senior year?*

At any rate, he is in this class with me and it is going to be unpleasant, to say the least. Blake has a way of getting under my skin. What really gets me is how popular he is with girls. I guess they like his dark hair, dark eyes, and that smoldering look he gets from his mother's side. She's Hispanic, or Latina, or whatever it is. The only time I ever see him smile—a kind of a surly smile, if you ask me—is when he's with girls. But even then, as with his wrestling, he has his limits. I've never seen Blake with one girl; he's always with a group. It's like he's using them as props. Or maybe he amuses them in some way. Why do girls like bad guys?

After about halfway through class, we're all sitting quietly, working on these problems. Ms. Emerson keeps the door open this day of all days, saying the room is getting a little warm. All of a sudden, we hear Johnny walking down the hall, singing that Michael Jackson song "Billie Jean."

The thing about Johnny and his singing is that it is apropos to nothing. It isn't like he heard that song on the radio that day, or like it is the anniversary of Michael Jackson's death or something. He just picks out songs from nowhere.

Johnny's assistant whispers, "Quiet, Johnny!" And everyone, including the teacher, is laughing, because as soon as she whispers, "Quiet," he sings even louder. "But the kid is not my son."

Ms. Emerson explains that the autism room is just down the hall and sometimes "you can hear them being different."

"Great, just what we need for a precalc class." I hear Blake's voice over my right shoulder. I wanted to punch him. But this other kid tells him he's being a douche, which takes some of the sting out. I know I've been mean to Johnny. But he is my brother, and even if he wasn't, I wouldn't ever say anything like that about a disabled kid.

"Hey, Ms. Emerson," one kid says, "were you around when Michael Jackson was big?"

She smiles coyly. "I was learning quadratic equations when *Thriller* came out. In other words, I was the tender age of four."

"Really?" another kid asks.

"All right, back to work!" she says with a smile. As she looks back down at her work, she starts mouthing to herself the guitar rift from the song: "Buh-ba-ba *ba* baba-bah! Buh-ba-ba *ba* baba-bah!" She keeps going, bopping her head to the beat until she looks up and realizes everyone is looking at her. Then everyone starts laughing.

I get the impression Ms. Emerson is the kind of math teacher who I know I'm going to like personally but will have a hard time explaining math to kids like me, who find math to be an alien language.

Elizabeth finds me in the cafeteria at lunch and insists on sitting with me, which is okay. The guys I'm sitting with are Chris and Jeff, who were in a couple of classes with me last year. They keep me from having to be alone among clusters of students.

"How's your first day going so far?" I ask her after I introduce everybody.

"It's okay," Elizabeth says. "I've got dance practice after school, you know."

"Yeah? How's that going?" I pull out my ham sandwich and apple from my brown bag.

"Miss Rosemary tells me she wants to work out a mini solo for me in the routine we're taking to the state championships. It ends at five. I know wrestling can go on much later, so I guess I'll sit somewhere and do homework until you're finished." She takes a bite of an apple.

"Is that all you're going to eat?" Chris asks.

"I can't let myself get weighed down!"

"Dancing is a lot like wrestling," I tell him, "always having to watch your weight."

"Glad I don't do sports," Chris says, chomping on his sandwich. It is a familiar refrain of his and Jeff's.

"I think I'll go visit Johnny's classroom at lunch tomorrow," she says, changing the subject. "It's the same period as we have."

"You're not going to meet people there," I chide a little. "What about the girls on the dance team?"

"Quit trying to run my life, Benjamin!" she snaps.

"I'm just trying to help," I snap back and leave it at that. *Why are girls so moody sometimes?* I think to myself.

That Friday, the main office calls my second-period teacher ten minutes before class is over to come pick up some bags. They turn out to be my wrestling shoes and lunch bag that I accidentally left in Mom's car. I see J. T. walking from the assistant principal's office.

"Hey, Ben." He smiles. "How's it going?"

"Pretty good, how 'bout you?" J. T. is a nice guy. I wish we had more in common, but overall, he's one of the few guys on the wrestling team I can halfway have a conversation with.

"Almost got my ass kicked for nothing! I mean suspended!"
"Why?"

"Because of Mrs. Ogilvy, you know, the French teacher?"

"Yeah?" My interest is piqued.

"We had this black kid from France come in our class. He's an exchange student or something. So I say—just trying to be conversational—'Wow, I guess there really are niggas in Paris.' You know the Kanye West song? Everybody laughed, but Mrs. Ogilvy didn't get it. She freaks out! *J. T.!*' She turns all red. You know what I'm talking about, don't ya, Ben? Kanye West?"

"Yeah, J. T., I've heard that song plenty of times in practice." I'm more into alternative music than rap, but I don't have much of a say in what is on the stereo in the wrestling room.

"Yeah, right. So anyway, she sends me up to Mr. Strong's office, and I'm thinking, 'I'm getting suspended for this?' Luckily, he just laughed and said to be more sensitive next time. Good thing Mr. Strong is a brotha. He gets it."

"Yeah," I say, trying not to laugh at J. T.'s attempts to sound cool. "Well, I'm glad you're okay."

"Coach would kill me if I missed wrestling practice 'cause I was suspended!" He looks terrified at the thought.

"Yeah, well, better not let the hall patrol see us loitering!" We both roll our eyes and smile. "I'll see you at practice today." I turn to go.

"See ya, Ben,"

"Hey, Ben." He runs back to me. "I'm having a party at my house tomorrow night. It's with my church's youth group, but anyone can come. We're trying to get people to come, you know, who don't go to church and stuff. But no pressure. You wanna come?"

It isn't like my social calendar is full, and I appreciate J. T. throwing me a bone. "Sure. What time?"

"Around six. Bring your bathing suit."

"Thanks, J. T."

Chapter 12

I get to J. T.'s house sometime after six that Saturday. There are a bunch of cars parked along the street and in his driveway. The neighbor is really nice but not super posh or anything. He lives in a community that has a golf course. I pass by the community playground and pool area.

I recognize Mike Duhon's red Fiesta first thing. It's parked next to the mailbox, leaving just enough room to keep any other cars from getting too close to his. Mike and I wrestled at the same weight, but he's moved up by ten pounds. I have always felt rather inferior to him, not as a wrestler but because girls drool over him. I stay in the car after I've already turned off the ignition. I'm a little nervous, to be honest. I'm not good at parties. Not that I'm a wallflower. I think I do try and mingle, but I wonder if people are really interested in me. I tend to get self-conscious. But I'm trying to correct that. So here goes.

A boy I don't know answers the door. "Come on in," he says with a plastic cup in his hands. "J. T.'s out by the pool. I'm just the bouncer!" He smiles.

"I'm Ben," I introduce myself.

"Gary," he says and goes on back to the kitchen. I start fighting my social anxiety. *Relax, Ben.*

I look around for people I know. There are a few kids around the table in the dining room right off the foyer, picking at some food. I head outside to find J.T. at the grill, flipping hamburgers.

There's some kids in the pool and J.T. is looking relaxed and joking around with people I don't know.

"Hey, Ben." He smiles. "Hey, everyone, this is Ben."

I get a polite "Hi" from the grill group, and then they go back to talking about some trip they all went on. Lots of insider jokes. So after a few minutes I head back inside.

I can't put my finger on it. I mean, what do I know? But I realize I could pick up a lot of pointers from J. T., as far as getting ahead socially. One thing I notice is that he smiles so easily. He is like Rosie in that way—he just sits, pants a little, and grins. That's what makes him approachable, to guys and girls. Everyone likes him.

That's why there are so many people at the party. I recognize several kids from school, including a couple from the wrestling team. I'm surprised to see Mike Duhon and Zack. They're seniors this year and definitely not the churchy type. They are part of the "in crowd" on the team. Those are the kids who get high and talk about who they had sex with. Mike and I were practice partners last year but he's moved up in size. J. T. is a little bit of a nerd like me in that way, because he's not into that. But people still accept him.

Almost everyone else is out by the pool. I'm sitting on his family room sofa with two other kids who are in a conversation. A girl is sitting in one of the chairs opposite. She looks uncomfortable, like she has social anxiety. She's pretty, with long dark brown hair and an angular face. I've become quite a student of faces and their shapes, as though the shapes tell the story of the person's life. Hers is a pretty face, with prominent eyes, which are emerald in color and seem to have a story going on behind them.

"How do you know J. T.?" I ask her.

"Oh." She looks at me as though she just notices me, as though she is deep in thought. "I don't really. I know Sammi, who knows J. T., I think from church. Sammi and I go to Adele High School."

"Oh, the Panthers," I say the obvious.

"Is it? The Panthers?" She smiles. "I'm new here anyway. Military brat."

"Marine?"

She nods. "My father got a position at the Pentagon. So we are supposed to be here for a few years at least."

"Well, Adele is a good school. I'm kind of new here, as well. I moved here about two years ago. I go to North Central."

"The other high school here," she says, as if she's trying to get her bearings.

"Yeah," I say. "It's a good school too. We have a good wrestling team, one of the best in the state."

"Are you a wrestler?" she asks politely.

"Yes." I appreciate that she asked. "Our football team is pretty good too. But Adele beats us at football. At least they have for the last year or two."

"I don't follow football," she says with reluctance. "I'm kind of a bookworm."

"What are you reading?"

She lights up and talks about all the books she has read. "Right now, I'm into *The Lord of the Rings* trilogy. I try to alternate between a new book and a classic."

"Did you see the movie?" I haven't read the book, but I've seen the movie, which, to be honest, was hard for me to follow.

"Not yet," she said. "I'm not sure I want to until I finish the books. The books are always better."

"Yeah, that's true," I say. I tell her I like the alternative history books by Harry Turtledove and the science fiction books by Orson Scott Card. She nods politely. I get the sense she's kind of shy and would like to talk more.

"I've read *Fahrenheit 451*," she says. "That's the only science fiction book I've read. I thought it was a good book, though."

"Yeah, I read that too." I nod. Now we're both smiling. She adjusts herself in the chair, likes she's starting to get comfortable. I sit forward, putting my elbows on my knees.

"Did you have to read that book? For a class, I mean?"

"Well, yeah," she admits, "but I still liked it."

"I'm Ben, by the way."

"I'm Emily." We both nod slightly, and there's a slight pause before I ask her if she wants to get something to eat.

"Sure." She smiles and stands up. She has a nice figure.

We go to the dining room, where the table is filled with all kinds of chips, veggie and fruit plates, brownies, and cookies. As we both fill up our plates, I look out the window and see Mike Duhon and Zack getting into Mike's car with some girls. I guess they have other, more exciting places to go. I'm not a part of that world, so I can only imagine.

"I guess it's kind of tough being in the military, having to move around so much," I say as I'm circling the smorgasbord.

"Yeah, I suppose so." Emily shrugs. "But it's all I've known. Different kids deal with it in different ways. I've always dealt with it by sticking my nose in a book!" She smiles apologetically.

"Well, I suppose there are worse ways of dealing with it." We get some drinks from the kitchen and go back to our seats in J. T.'s den. "Is it hard to make friends? I guess you get asked that question all the time."

She looks thoughtfully. "Sometimes it's hard. My father doesn't always move like a lot of people do, where it's every two years or so. Sometimes he has gotten orders to leave after only a few months!"

"Wow, that's gotta be tough." I am starting to relax with her now.

She shrugs. "Well, it is what it is. Oh God, I hate that phrase, and here I just said it! Anyway, I mean I've learned to accept whatever comes my way."

"That's a good way to look at things."

"I'm a junior this year, so I guess this is where I will be graduating!" She smiles. *I hope so*, I'm thinking. We continue talking, mostly about books, but it gets us talking about other things—which characters we like and why, places we dream about visiting, and our personal philosophies about life. That's what books do.

It's almost nine. We go out to the pool for a while and talk with some other kids, including J. T. and Sammi. I ask Emily if I can get her phone number, and she says sure. So I text her my number, and she texts me hers. My phone vibrates. She gave me her number. Her *real* number.

"It was nice talking to you," she says as she walks out with Sammi.

"Yeah, nice talking to you too," I say. I think she really means it.

Chapter 13

If I count Jason's sister to dance back in middle school, this girl who is in my freshman history class, and another girl in my youth group, this would be the fourth time I have asked a girl out on a date. If Emily says yes, it'll be a first. (I don't count that "date" with Maddie at the beach as a real date. That was totally orchestrated by Christy.)

I wait almost a week to text Emily.

"Hi Emily. This is Ben. Just wondering how U R doing."

I thought for a few minutes before sending it. I changed the "U R" to "you are," thinking about what she said about not liking the phrase "It is what it is." Maybe she's a stickler for spelling too. But I finally hit send. And wait.

I wait for ten minutes before my phone vibrates.

"Hi Ben. Doing well. How about you? Just finished some math homework."

I take it as a good sign, so I cut to the chase.

"Would you like to go see a movie this weekend?"

I get a text quickly back.

"Which movie?"

Then I get another one right after that.

"Oh! I would be happy to go to any movie."

Then another.

"Well, not any movie!"
Then a final one.

"Please call."

So I give her a call. It's kind of awkward at first. We say hi to each other like we're strangers. We get to "How ya doing?" and "How's school going?" and begin warming up to each other again immediately.

"So do you like to go to movies?" I ask casually.

"Actually, I don't see a lot of movies." She laughs nervously. I'm unsure if she's trying to blow me off, so I walk things back.

"Would you like to go to Sergeants for drinks? And food?" I add after realizing how dumb having drinks at Sergeants sounds. Sergeants is just a local diner where they have pictures of different sergeants from old TV shows and movies. But it's a good start.

"Oh yeah, I'd love to," she says in a sincere tone. "Sorry, I didn't mean to sound like I was blowing you off. Sorry, I hate that phrase."

"Yeah, that's okay," I say lightheartedly. She gives me her address, and I tell her I will pick her up at seven.

Elizabeth goes with me to the mall that afternoon. Ostensibly, we're getting her some new clothes, but I need some myself and I didn't want Mom to go with me. She doesn't know what looks good. Elizabeth loves picking out clothes, so I put her to use.

"You need to wear these." She hands me some shirts. "And these!" She tosses me some jeans. She's really having fun, and it's kind of a relief seeing her happy for a change. She's been neurotic ever since she was selected for the dance team. It's been that "Do I look fat?" crap ever since she got the dance outfit or uniform or whatever they call it. Maybe it's just nerves she's working out, being out on the football field at halftime and shaking her butt in front of hundreds of people.

I take a shower, shave what little hair is on my face, and get dressed. I go downstairs as everyone else is sitting down at the kitchen table to eat dinner. Before I grab the keys, I ask Mom if she can transfer some more money to my debit card. She looks at me like she's about to give me a lecture but then says okay.

"Have a good time," she says. "You are taking the Acura, right?"

"Yes," I say as I head out the door. Dad just bought an Acura sedan that looks really cool. It's the car they let me use on such occasions as these.

"Don't do anything I wouldn't do!" Dad cracks.

Emily lives in a subdivision south of where we live. I'm not too familiar with this part of town, and that adds to my nervousness. On top of that there is her father, who is a marine colonel or something. But I get to her house and ring the doorbell, and things go okay. Her mother opens the door. Emily comes down the stairs. She looks very pretty. Her hair looks shiny, like in those hair commercials, and she's got on more makeup than she did at J. T.'s party. She looks happier too, which makes me happy.

Her father comes into the foyer and gives a quick handshake. Her mother is very nice and tells us to have a good time. It's like this is the first time for all of us. And I'm thinking, *She's so pretty. How could she not have a boyfriend?*

We get to Sergeants, and the hostess takes us to a booth. The waitress comes to get our drink orders and takes off. The walls of Sergeants are filled with famous sergeants: Bilko, York, Schultz, and others. They're mostly old black-and-white photographs. It gives us something to talk about.

"This is a neat concept." She looks around. "I didn't realize there were so many famous sergeants!" She smiles at me rather reservedly. Her shoulders are hunched in protection mode.

"Yeah, it's kind of weird." I crinkle my brow. "I mean, usually the idea of food and army personnel don't mix!"

"Well"—she laughs as she points to the rotund Sergeant Schultz from *Hogan's Heroes*—"that sergeant looks as if he knows a thing or two about food!" She pauses for a second. "I like these old TV shows and movies. Sorry I'm not much into going to movies playing in the theaters. I watch the classic movie channel. My mother is really into all those old movies. Both of my parents are, actually. I'm more into books. I guess you've figured out I'm a real geek."

"Don't sell yourself short, Emily," I say, a little annoyed. *If you're such a geek, why would I want to go out with you? I mean, what would that make me? Don't answer that, Ben!* "You just seem a little shy, that's all."

"Yeah." She looks up as the waitress brings us our drinks. We pull the wrappers off the straws, put them in our glasses, and drink. I am figuring out what to say next. She stares at the crinkled straw wrappers on the table. The waitress stands over us. She's tall with the build of an athlete.

"Have you all had the chance to look at our specials?" the waitress, who looks like she's working to put herself through college, asks us with a big sisterly, "Don't you two look cute" tone. "We have the Sergeants special, which is a tender roast cooked to perfection, stacked on a pile of potatoes with vegetables on the side. It's really good."

"Would you recommend it?" I try to sound in command of the conversation.

"Sure." The waitress shrugs.

"What else would you recommend?" I study the plastic four-page menu briefly and look over the top of the menu to study Emily's face for her thoughts.

"Everything's good at Sergeants," the waitress says, as if she's trying to hurry us along even though the restaurant doesn't look that busy. "We have really good salads." She looks over at Emily with a smile. "Should I give you both a few more minutes?"

"Sure." I give her a nod, an indication that she's dismissed. We both look at each other like we're trying not to laugh.

"I guess she thinks we're kind of cute!" Emily grins.

"We don't look that young," I protest. "Do we?"

"I probably look like an awkward adolescent." Emily studies the menu. "It's my go-to look."

"Well, I guess I'm a little shy too." I try to figure out my next line while staring at the menu. "I've decided on getting the Sergeant York bone-in steak with french fries." I want to show Emily that she doesn't have to go cheap with me.

"Oh, wow." She raises her eyebrows and then lowers them again to contemplate her order. "I think I'll get … the salad. With grilled chicken strips!" She gives me a relaxed smile and closes her menu. "You don't seem shy." She looks at me with some consideration. "You don't seem afraid of what people think. That's nice."

"Thanks." I smile back, not knowing where to take the conversation. I mean, how interesting can being shy be? So I go back to books. "I'm reading Andrew Klavan's *The Last Thing I Remember*. Ever heard of Andrew Klavan?"

"No, but that doesn't mean anything." She sits up a little straighter. "I bet I know what it's about, though. Don't tell me: a kid who gets kidnapped by aliens or government thugs or something and has to find a way to escape."

"Well, yeah." I smile. "It's something like that, but it's really good. I guess there are lots of young adult books out about that kind of stuff."

"Yeah, all these books about forces beyond our control, dystopias, and alienation. I hate that word." She emphasizes the word *hate*, and a look of hurt and anger clouds her face.

"You must have a list of words and phrases you hate. 'Alienation' and 'it is what it is' are two you've told me so far." I observe her like I'm her therapist. "Oh, and what was the phrase you used on the phone? 'Blowing you off.'" She turns slightly red, but I grin. "So why do you hate the word 'alienation'?"

"Well," she begins slowly, "when I was in sixth grade I got called the Alien by this group of girls on my bus. Then everyone started calling me that. I still wore these big dark-rimmed glasses, and the lenses were the glass bottle kind, the kind that make your eyes look like saucers. To top it off, I had braces. My teeth were stuck out to here." She puts her thumb up to her lips. "I got called that all throughout middle school."

"Aw, that's terrible." *So now everything's starting to make sense. She still thinks she's ugly.*

"I was so happy when my father got orders to move. I hated being called the Alien!"

"Well, you must be from the planet Urhotness!" I smile at her.

She giggles. I am glad to see her laugh, and I'm even happier that I can make her laugh. "Yeah, middle school is a hard time."

"It has helped that I no longer wear braces and I now wear contacts. I just got them. I've worn glasses all my life, and I was reluctant to try contacts. My mother started pushing me to get them. It still feels a little strange. I still reach up to adjust my glasses and realize I'm not wearing them!" She looks at me briefly with a closed-mouth smile and continues. "Yeah, but my last high school wasn't so bad." She looks over at the salt and pepper shakers, not smiling. "People there were okay. I probably should have put myself out there more, but I kind of kept to myself. Just going to school and babysitting."

Sensing that she regrets saying too much about her insecurities, I put myself out there now. "I hate it when people call me Roundhead."

"Who calls you that?" She wrinkles her forehead.

"This kid on my wrestling team. He's a senior."

"That's so dumb! It's not even creative!" She shakes her head with distain at Blake's sheer lack of verbal prowess. "At least Alien shows some thought behind it. But Roundhead? What does that even mean?"

"That I have a roundish head, like a ball." Now I'm starting to look embarrassed. I really put myself out there. But maybe my round head is like the elephant in the living room; sooner or later, you have to talk about it.

She bursts out laughing. "Sorry, I don't mean to laugh, but that's so stupid. Your head isn't even round!" She wrinkles her nose. "You have a face like Ernest Hemingway. I guess you could say he had a roundish face. Somewhat. I don't know."

"He had more of a square head," I opine. "My last year's English teacher had a poster of Hemingway on her wall. He definitely had a square face." I'm starting to grow more confident as I discover my head is starting to take on a new shape. "He looked like a giant—Hemingway, I mean."

"Very distinctive-looking," she says, looking confidently at me. "And you have that same type of face!"

"So now my face is starting to get some angles to it?" I chuckle.

"Yeah." She starts laughing with me. "It matches my triangle face. I've learned to live with that." She nods in satisfaction. "I'm okay with my head."

"You have a nice face, Emily. Has anyone told you that?"

She shrugs off my compliment. "Let's face it, Ben. We're just different. Distinctive-looking! The way people used to look in a bygone era: Betty Davis, Clark Gable, Robert Mitchum. Before everyone had the same plastic surgeon who gave everyone the same face!"

There's a brief silence that makes her uncomfortable, so she says, "I don't mean to go on about *that*!"

So I try to segue the conversation back to books. "I think that's why I'm a reader. I'm more into my head—I mean, into my mind. It's great to have books that just take you somewhere else."

"*The Lord of the Rings* definitely takes you somewhere else, but honestly, I'm not much of a fantasy and science fiction reader." She thinks for a second. "Well, I just grab what appeals to me. If it feels real, like there's something I can get from it, I'll read any book."

"Okay." The waitress arrives with a big tray of our food. "I have the Sergeant York"—she immediately sets it in front of me—"and the first-class salad with chicken strips." She sets it down in front of Emily and asks if there's anything else.

"We're good." I give her a grin, and she tells us to "Enjoy!"

We unroll the silverware from the napkins and start to eat. She takes a bite and then says, "I just read *The Sun Also Rises* by Hemingway before I got started on *Lord of the Rings*. Have you read any of his books?"

"No, but that's on the list in honors English this year." I pour some ketchup on my fries and start to dig into my steak.

"I don't recommend it." She pats her mouth with her napkin. "I know we're supposed to like Hemingway, but I didn't get it."

"What's it about?" I take a bite of my steak.

"Just this guy named Jake and a woman named Brett." She pushes the lettuce around with her fork. "They're in Paris. They sit in cafés and talk and drink. That's about it. Oh, there's bullfighting in Spain too."

"Other than the bullfight, we could write about talking and drinking." I take a sip of my Coke and then concede, "Well, we could write about drinking Coke and water!" She nods with a big bite from her salad in her mouth. "The bullfight is probably the big thing in the book, I guess."

She nods, wiping a little ranch dressing from the side of her mouth. "It's supposed to be about how bad things got after World War I. Loss of innocence, loss of purpose. Stuff like that."

"Oh." I shrug. "I guess that's supposed to be deep."

"Yeah, I know," she agrees. "It's like, well, the sun rises, and the same stuff happens over and over. Like it's always going to be that way. Nothing new. It's kind of depressing."

"Sounds like it," I say. "Why do English teachers make us read boring stuff?"

"I heard *The Old Man and the Sea* is good," Emily says with more enthusiasm. "I promised one of my Goodreads friends, who's a big Hemingway fan, that I'd give it a try." She paused. "Will you read it?"

"I'll give it a try." I feel illiterate compared to Emily. But I am glad to talk to a reader. "I'm more into contemporary writers." I try to sound sophisticated.

"Why do so many writers today write about dystopias? Like *The Hunger Games* and *Divergent*. And *The Giver*! Remember that one? It's like our generation is afraid of something happening. Something out there. Something beyond our control."

We are quiet for a few seconds, taking that last part in. Then she says quietly, "I think we're afraid of connecting. I know I am."

"Me too." Then I say, "I know with me, it's how my parents are all eaten up by politics and how the government is out to get control of everything. It drives me nuts sometimes!"

She laughs. "Yeah, my parents are like that too, although my father tries not to talk about it. He has to be neutral when it comes to politics. He never says who he voted for. But I've got a pretty good idea. My mother? Definitely know where she is on the issues!"

"Maybe we should give them a copy of *The Sun Also Rises*. Then maybe they'll realize the world has always been in a mess. So lighten up, folks!" She smiles.

We take a few bites of our dinner. I'm trying to be aware of not smacking when I eat. Mom says I tend to smack when I'm eating. Emily swallows and tells me, "You know I only have sixty-four friends on Facebook?" She takes a sip of her drink.

"That's not many in the grand scheme of things," I say. "Most kids have hundreds. Actually, I don't even go on Facebook much anymore. I just text mostly."

"Oh." She looks embarrassed. "I'm so out of what's going on. My parents were always kind of strict about going online and all that. But it's okay. I'm not good at being social, as you can see."

"You're fine!" I almost get irritated at the shrinking violet routine. I make myself a mental note that I am going to have to work with her on that.

"Well," she says hesitantly, "can I friend you anyway?"

"I don't want to be that kind of friend, Emily. Not to you." I look at her straight in the eye. "Do you know what I mean?"

She looks a little confused, and then something pops into her head. "You don't want to be a Jake to my Brett!" She looks alarmed.

"What do you mean?" I give her a wary look.

"Nothing," she says. "Anyway, I don't want to be Brett either. I'm not that kind of girl."

"I just don't want to get friend-zoned." I give her a warning look.

"Sammi used that same phrase!" Emily says animatedly. "I guess you could say Jake was friend-zoned."

"Well, *I* hate that phrase!" I say pointedly.

"Well, I certainly don't picture you in that area!" She looks at me with affection. "Ben, I hope you'll text me again," she says quickly. Then she looks down at her plate. "I mean, well, you know."

"Yeah, I know," I tell her.

The check comes, and she looks at it like she's unsure of whether she should take it. She starts to reach for it.

"Hey, I have that!" I smile as I pick up the check.

"Oh, I'm sorry!" She turns a little red. "I didn't mean … I just never know who …"

"Don't worry, I don't have T. rex arms!" I grin as I get out my wallet.

"T. rex arms?" She looks at me quizzically.

"It's a saying in my family when someone holds up their forearms with their elbows at their sides." I imitate Aunt Terry. "'I would pick up the check but I can't reach it!'"

She laughs, and I start laughing. I'm glad I can make her laugh.

I drive her home. We continue to talk about things that are going on in our lives, mostly school. She admits that she tried out for the field hockey team in her last school but didn't make it.

"I wasn't fast enough." She sighs. "So my father insisted that I get on some kind of rec team. I'm still not a good player! I know I need to show some way to stand out, you know, when it comes to applying for college." She sighs again and fold hers arms.

"Hey, next week, let's go see a movie." I'm really confident that she will say yes now. "At the movie theater."

She looks at me with a grin. "Okay, sure! I'm not that much of a hermit, Ben!"

"So is there anything you'd like to see?" I ask, looking at her as if she is a little puppy I just found and want to take home and cuddle with.

"You decide!" she says with a satisfied look on her face. Then she lights up with another idea. "You know, I've never been to a homecoming game. Have you?"

"No, I'm not much into high school football," I say as a way of excuse, but that's not the real reason, of course. The real reason is that I don't want to see how everyone else is matched up but me. "But my sister is on the dance team this year, so I'm kind of obligated to go to some games."

"Maybe we can go to the homecoming game at your school," she suggests enthusiastically, and for the first time I get enthusiastic about going to homecoming. She pauses to await my response.

"Yeah," I say casually, "we could even go to the dance afterward. If you want."

"Sure!" she blurts out and then adds, "If you want to. Whatever." She lets out a big sigh, and I know what she's going to say. "I hate that word!" We say it in unison and start laughing.

I pull into her driveway and shut off the engine. I look at her with uncertainty, and she gives me the same look.

"I'll walk you to your door," I tell her finally. We both get out of the car at the same time and head for the front door.

"I really had a good time, Ben." She smiles shyly. I take that as a green light to give her a kiss. I'm not so practiced at this, and before I talk myself out of it, I decide to rush ahead, which causes me to head bump her.

"Oh, God, I'm sorry." I panic until I realize she's laughing.

"It's okay," she says. Then, going a little more slowly, I reach over and kiss her. She doesn't back off. She likes me. And I like her.

I can't sleep that night. Not that that is a bad thing.

Sunday is usually a mixed day. I'm glad I get to sleep in a little before going to church, but I dread having to go back to school on Monday. Today is different. I have a smile I'm trying to keep to myself.

It is now afternoon, and Dad and Mom sit on the couch with Rosie lying between them. Mom blogs on her laptop as Dad reads the Sunday paper while catching up on their dose of Fox News shows. I'm in the kitchen with Elizabeth, fixing lunch.

"Benjamin must have had a good time last night," Dad tells Mom in a serious tone. "I looked at his phone and saw that he texted that girl a picture of his junk!"

"Dad!" I'm halfway laughing and halfway annoyed that he's making a big deal about my date.

"What?" Mom gasps and stops typing.

"Yeah, he texted her a picture of his *room*!" Dad says with a straight face.

There's a slight pause before they both start guffawing.

"Oh, that's funny, Dad." I roll my eyes and shake my head.

"Don't let her get a whiff of your wrestling clothes! Whew!" Mom wrinkles her nose as they continue to laugh.

"Thanks, Mom!" *Is that supposed to be funny?*

"I'm just kidding." Mom looks as if she has realized she went a bit overboard on the teasing. "She is a lucky girl."

"Thanks, Mom." But I have to admit, I did start thinking a little bit more about the mess in my room. Not that Emily would ever go there—in real life, that is. I used to figure every guy had a messy room. Seth's room was a mess. So was Brian's. The only guys who had really neat rooms were gay. Mom always watched those decorating shows on HGTV, so she of all people should know that.

Still, for the first time, I have someone to clean up for. I made sure my door was closed so they couldn't see that I was gathering up all the dirty clothes across my room.

Chapter 14

It's almost too good to be true. I have a girl to text to every day, just to say hello, without that feeling of dread coming over me that she won't text back. I've passed the point where I worry about rejection; we've been out on two other dates since our first one. *Of course she likes me! Get it through your head!*

We're playing Adele High, but she agrees to sit with me and my parents. "It's not like I'm really into the school spirit thing yet, anyway!" she tells my parents. We sit in the stands. At halftime, there's the band and, of course, the dance team. I see Elizabeth second from the left in the second row of three rows.

"She should really be in the front," Mom says, annoyed. "She's much too good to be in the back."

"Look at the girl next to her," Dad counters. "She's kind of chunky to be out there in that skimpy outfit. I know I'm going to get flak for that—beauty comes in all shapes and sizes, but really."

"Big butts are in, Dad," I tell him.

"Thanks to J.Lo and Kim Kardashian," Mom adds. "But some of their moves look awfully close to twerking. They're cutting it close."

"They're all good, though," Emily says. The dance team has always been one of the bright spots in the annals of North Central High's short history. They have placed number one in the state every year for the past five years. That's thanks in part to Rosemary Butler, who is the coach for the team and also has her own dance studio here in Adele. I guess that's something to brag about. At least they all do Adele.

"But Elizabeth is really good," Mom insists. "I'm not saying that just because I'm her mother, but, well, look at them! I'm no expert, but she's just got more technique."

"I agree," Dad says. "When you judge on talent, Elizabeth is one of the better ones. And talent should count for something."

Having talent and being judged on merit are big things for Dad these days. He talks a lot about how working for the government is rewarding in some ways, but as far as talent, the only kind that means anything is political talent. I guess he doesn't have much of that.

But he is good at what he does, being a numbers guy, making money (especially for other people). He has been getting his ducks all in a row, work-wise, to start his own business. He met up with his business associates in New York again this past week. The idea of being his own boss, or at least being a co-owner—having some skin in the game, as they call it—invigorates him.

"I can't stand being a government drone! The bureaucracy makes a person brain dead," he complains. "That's all that's in Washington, just a bunch of lemmings."

I lean over toward Emily and whisper in her ear, "Sorry about my father going off on a rant. He does that on occasion."

She laughs. "Don't worry about it. My father does the same thing!"

But the good thing, he assures us, is that the firm is set up so that he can work out of our house and commute every once in a while to New York. We won't have to move.

"With Elizabeth doing so well on the dance team, it would be a shame for us to leave," Mom said about Dad's new venture. She added as an aside, "And Benjamin is on a great wrestling team. And Johnny's doing well in school. They have a really good program." That is what matters most, that Johnny is in a good program. *Like any program would do him much good.* Of course, don't tell Mom that.

"That's so great!" Emily gushes as I explain to her about Dad's situation. "I hate that word, 'great.' I mean, I just think it's overused. But in this case, it fits." She looks at me and smiles. She really has a beautiful smile. It gets more beautiful every time I see her.

"Yeah." I put my arm around her and give her a squeeze. "Why don't we go sit down front?" I figure we've spent enough time with my parents and Johnny. Besides, I want to show her off and walk around the stands, the concession stand, anywhere I can see people I know from classes, especially the guys on the wrestling team.

The homecoming king and queen are selected. But I feel like Emily and I are the real king and queen. I was going to tell her how I feel, but something told me to hold back. Emily doesn't realize she isn't an ugly duckling anymore. To be honest, I want to keep it that way. I know that sounds selfish, but if she ever knows she is much prettier than the homecoming queen, she might move on to bigger and better things. I can't lose her now.

We are all smiles at the homecoming dance the next night. It isn't just for show either. "I'm so glad I'm here, Ben," she whispers to me as I hold her close in a slow dance. "I feel like I'm finally home."

"Me too."

"Don't make me have to go on suicide watch this year!" Coach Garlin growls at us at our first official practice.

Last year, the team placed only fourth in the state. North Central has been at least in the top three for the past ten years. Coach G took the humiliation pretty hard. But part of it is just because of the way he is. Coach G looks like a heart attack waiting to happen, so everyone treats him with kid gloves, hoping not to say anything that will set him off. He's a big guy, a little over six feet and hefty, not quite sumo size, with a red face and a swollen neck from all the years of working out.

"This year, we're leaving nothing to chance," he continues. "I've got some great assistants here." He extends his arm in back of him to introduce some new faces. "These guys have been past winners and have volunteered to help us out." Then he gets up and takes a deep breath. "But it's up to you! You don't put the work in, give 150 percent, then don't bother being here."

Coach G's pep talks are never peppy. They are more like threats peppered with guilt trips. "You guys who were on the varsity team last year, I hope you are angry, mad as hell that you didn't do it for North Central, for your team, for yourselves! Last year you got your asses beat. Except for a few of you who went out there and did what you were supposed to do—the rest of you looked so half-assed. That's not how it works here.

"Some of you who were on the varsity team last year won't make it this year. You all are going to have to fight for your spot. I've got some new kids this year who are hungry, have the fire in the belly. They want your spot. You juniors and seniors got your work cut out for you. Now get busy!"

Right now, I'm weighing in at 153. That's my walking-around weight. My wrestling weight last year was around 138, but I've grown some. I can't wrestle that weight, but I can definitely get down to 142. I'm going to have to compete with either J. T. for the 155, Mike Duhon for the 148, or Blake for the 142. We're all in a cluster of weight classes that form the most competitive in high school.

I get home from practice, and Dad as usual asks me how wrestling practice went. After supper, Dad goes down to the basement to watch the big screen while I help Mom clear the table.

"Are you going out with Emily this weekend?" she asks me when he's left.

113

"I haven't asked her yet, but I hope so," I say as I put all the condiments back in the fridge.

"You could invite her over for dinner here, you know," she says as she stacks dishes in the dishwasher. "You don't have to go out."

"Yeah, that's true," I answer offhandedly.

"I was also noticing," she said as she turned the hot water on to scrub the pans, "that several stores are hiring for holiday help. It might be good to earn some extra money—"

"Yeah." I close the refrigerator door and look for other things to put away.

"Now that you're going out more."

"Right." I hang up some dish towels on the oven door.

"Just saying." She shrugs.

I hate that phrase. *I know what you're saying, Mom!* Normally, I get annoyed with Mom's attempts at getting me to look for a job. She really doesn't get how time-consuming wrestling is on top of keeping up my grades. I don't have time for anything else if I am going to get better. But with Emily in the picture, I can see her point a little better. Maybe working a few days over the holidays would be a good thing.

"Yeah, you're right," I tell her. She turns around and looks at me, surprised. "I'll look into it. Thanks for dinner, Mom."

"You're welcome." She smiles, surprised again. I head down to the basement, where I have an old desk with my computer that I use to do homework. It's in a little alcove that's open to the big TV screen but far enough to keep me somewhat focused on my studies.

Dad sits in his big chair watching ESPN. "You know, Benjamin, and don't take this the wrong way," he says without turning his focus from the screen, "but you might not want to get too serious with a girl during wrestling season."

"Dad!" I protest. "That's not going to affect anything." I really don't want to have this conversation, especially when I see Elizabeth sitting on the sofa working on her homework."

"Tony Romo didn't do so well when he was with Jessica Simpson!" Dad says. I can't tell if he's being serious or not.

"Dad!" I throw my head back, rolling my eyes. "You're kidding, right?"

"But Tom Brady is still on top with Gisele Bündchen!" Elizabeth says.

Dad and I burst out laughing. "What?" Elizabeth has never been a person who gets innuendos. "Why are you laughing at me?"

"Well, touché, Elizabeth!" Dad roars. "But seriously, Benjamin, this is your year. I think you could be competitive in either 142 or 148. How's Mike Duhon looking?"

"He's good," I say. "He would be tough to beat." And it's true. Mike seems to have it all: a natural talent for wrestling, good grades (not at the very top but still competitive), good looks, and a girlfriend. How he can get away with smoking pot, I don't know. Some guys have all the luck. They don't have to try.

But, as I have been told so many times, life is not fair. Now that I have a girlfriend (and a good-looking one at that), I don't want to keep her a secret. I want to show her off in front of the guys on the wrestling team. I'm not the loser they think I am.

Chapter 15

Coach G gave us his brief pep talk about the tournament which will be in two days. To summarize, he said, "Don't embarrass me! You want to know how not to embarrass me? *Win!*"

"Can you go to the tournament this Saturday?" I text Emily while I'm ready to head out of the gym.

"I don't know anything about wrestling, Ben," Emily texts back noncommittally. "Besides, I have lots of homework."

I'm starting to feel a little nervous, like she's giving me the brush-off. So I try calling her. Thank God she answers. "Hi, Ben," she says cheerfully enough.

I cut to the chase. "Come on, Em, this would mean a lot to me if you went to see me this Saturday."

"Oh, well …" She sounds doubtful. "Is this just like that stuff they do on television? I hate violence. I'm sure that sounds stupid, but it's true."

"This isn't pro wrestling, Emily!" I say, irritated.

"Sorry," she says, mouse-like.

"Sorry?" I snap. I relent. "I just hate it when people get real wrestling mixed up with that fake stuff. It's a real sport. It's an Olympic sport. Tougher than football. I used to play football, so I know." I leave out when I played football, which was in fifth grade. I like her to think of me as a stud playing football, not as a kid.

"Sorry, Ben." She laughs warmly. "I'm hopeless when it comes to sports. But I appreciate the fact that you are a scholar/athlete."

"Yeah, well"—I turn a little pink—"don't expect a lot of scholars around here though!"

"Well, I can probably go for an hour or so. Is it going to be at North Central?"

"Yeah, it'll be going on all day," I tell her. "You can bring a book—in fact, I recommend it, or do your homework out in the cafeteria. It'll be right next to the gym. I'll call you when I'm ready to go on the mat."

"Okay, that sounds like that would work."

"You do want to see me, don't you?" It's good we're close enough that I can ask her a question and halfway expect an honest answer that is also a positive answer.

"Of course I do, Ben! Quit being so controlling!" she scolds me.

"Sorry, Emily," I say contritely. "I'm sorry. It just means a lot to me if you come and see me."

"You really like wrestling, don't you?"

"Yeah, I guess I do," I say, which means I have to go out there and impress her. "I'm not the best player," I say as a caveat. "Well, North Central is one of the best teams—one of the top teams—in the state."

"I bet you're good, Ben," she assures me. "And I like a guy who has a passion. It doesn't even matter what it is."

"Thanks, Emily."

"I'm glad it's not something gross, like deer hunting," she says with a tinge of anger. "I just hate to see my father gutting the poor things."

"Well, I'm glad you don't think wrestling is gross," I tell her, although I have no problem with deer hunting. I'm a big meat eater, though I stick with beef.

The bus is already there when Dad drops me off at the school parking lot at six in the morning. It's still dark. So goes wrestling season. I get on the bus, still as anxious to see Emily in the bleacher seats as I am to wrestle the kid from Rappahannock Valley. We've wrestled each other for two years now. He and I are as evenly matched as two wrestlers can be.

It isn't until we get to the gym that we find out when our match starts. I look on the wall where they put the schedule up. I text Emily and tell her my match doesn't start until ten. Until then, I warm up just enough to get my muscles awake, and then I pull out a book from my gym bag, take out the small blanket protected by the plastic trash liner Mom put it in, and proceed to relax until an hour before my match is supposed to start.

I'm wrestling Adam Stafford, who has really good footwork. When a wrestler has good footwork, it's hard to grab him for a throw. The good thing about me is my upper body strength. I've got pretty good arms and shoulders. I hope they work this time.

Adam and I shake hands and get into position. He's got the green ankle bracelet strapped on; I have the red. He immediately starts dancing around while I look for an opportunity to take an arm or leg. Adam likes to get his opponent dancing in a circle with him, but I don't fall for it. He moves to my left and I suddenly turn and grab his arm, but he swings out of it.

It isn't until the third round that he gets a little worn out from all the dancing. Adam wins by being an escape artist, but I'm not letting it happen. I hop back and forth from one leg to the other, just standing there until the opportunity comes. He grabs my waist, but I'm able to reach underneath his arms and turn him around. His footwork fails him, and he falls to the floor. I score two points for the takedown, the only numbers either of us puts up.

Emily is standing up, clapping happily as the ref raises my hand as the victor. I was hoping for a pin to show her I am at the top of my game, but with Adam, that is unrealistic. Still, I look up at her and smile. She waves to me and blows me a kiss. I am hoping everyone sees that. Here is geeky Ben, victorious on the mat and off.

"To be honest, Ben, I had a hard time following how you keep score on these matches," she tells me as I wipe myself off with a towel. "But it was clear for anyone to see you dominated that match."

"Well, there's one more to go." I take a swig from my water bottle. "It's for first place. It won't be for a while. Would you like to go to the cafeteria and have something to eat?"

"Sure," she says. "I got some of my homework done, but it's awfully hard to concentrate sometimes. It's really noisy in here." It's hard to forget sometimes how noisy these tournaments are until a novice spectator points it out. To me, it is white noise; I just tune it out.

It turns out how I predicted: the kid from Rappahannock, Zack Gunn, is my rival for first place. I'm trying not to psych myself out by having Emily here put so much pressure on me. Dad is here too, as usual, and usually, I am able to tune him out. But Emily is another matter.

"If you want to go now, I understand," I tell her as we are in line for pizza slices. "It's a long time between matches, and it must be hard to sit around."

Emily looks relieved but also tries to hide it. "Are you sure?"

"Sure, I can call you when I'm about to wrestle again, and you can come back." She acts reluctant but accepts my offer.

"Be sure to let me know when you're about to wrestle," she presses me. "I'm proud of you, Ben! I wish I could do something that you could be proud of me for."

"Just like yourself more, Emily. Stop with the self-deprecation all the time." I try not to sound too unkind, but it gets on my nerves. "What is it about girls? Either they're snapping away pictures of themselves on Snapchat, or they hate everything about themselves."

"We're all insecure, I guess." Emily is able to take a step back and analyze things. I like that, and when I tell her so, she gives me a big smile.

We kiss each other good-bye in front of the glass doors that lead to the parking lot. "I'll see you soon!" she whispers as she gives me one last hug before she takes off.

I win my next match seven to five. I get a gold medal, but they give out awards so late at these things that I tell Emily not to wait around. "I'm so proud of you!" she tells me again. I'm on top of the world.

Things are really serious when someone meets your family. I know Emily and I are taking our relationship to the next level when we spend time at each other's homes. To be honest, the only time I ever felt that feeling of "my home is your home" has been with Seth and a little bit with Brian, although it only pertained to the basement, where we would spend a majority of the time playing video games.

Having dinner with her parents is more nerve-racking than any wrestling match I've ever had, especially with her deer-hunting father. I get the feeling there is a lot of distance between the two, and I am hoping to help her close that. I mean, I know my father can be a little hard, especially when it comes to wrestling and grades ("Why is this a B and not an A?"). And her father is a marine through and through.

"So Emily tells me you're a wrestler," he says as he comes to the dinner table last. We all sit there with our hands on our laps, practically immobile, as if we're waiting for the ref to blow the whistle, indicating the match has begun.

"Yes, sir." I punctuate a lot of my sentences with "sir." Good thing I started out life in Texas, where it comes naturally.

"Are you a good wrestler?" he challenges me.

"I've won a couple of tournaments." I make my case. "North Central has some of the best wrestlers in the state, so it's hard—"

"What about any state championships?" He continues riding me hard. "There's a bunch of tournaments going on all the time, at least there was when I was in high school back in Pennsylvania."

"Pennsylvania has some of the best wrestling in the country." I take the bowl of rice Emily's mother hands me and dish up some on my plate. Her father grunts in acknowledgment of my last statement, and we eat in silence. Then he turns to me and looks me straight in the eyes.

"Are you a fighter, son?"

"Yes, sir," I say, not quite fast enough for his liking.

"'Cause if you're not a fighter, then don't bother with it. You understand, son?" I dare not turn from his stare.

"Yes, sir." I'm frozen. He's frozen. We're all locked in our positions. Then he breaks out in a big grin and slaps me on the back. "You'll do all right, Ben." It's the first time he calls me by my name. I guess I'm okay. I look over at Emily, who looks at me with slight embarrassment but a shy grin.

Later, she tells me she thinks her father likes me. "I want to stay on his good side," I say with relief. Her mother, on the other hand, is just the opposite—very warm and gracious, always asking if I would like more this or that. Talk about good cop, bad cop. I like Emily (dare I say love?), but I can't wait for the evening to be over. But then, she has to deal with my family.

We are driving on the street that leads to the street where I live, when we see Elizabeth jogging by. I honk the horn at her and wave as I'm driving by. She gives me an annoyed look.

"That's Elizabeth." I shake my head. "She's into running these days. At least it's something else besides that stupid dance stuff she does."

"Well, that's dedication, running when it's so cold out," Emily says and defends her dancing. "I think it's great that she can dance. I just hope she's not like a lot of girls who are into that."

"Stuck-up, you mean?" I ask her as I'm about to make a right turn.

"Yeah." Emily sighs. "Maybe it's a stereotype, but girls on cheerleading squads or dance teams"—she shakes her head—"they're just mean. Or maybe they're just into themselves too much."

"Well, she can be that way," I warn her. "But don't let her get to you. Just put her in her place. That's what I try to do."

Later, she and Elizabeth strike up a conversation that lasts for a while. I'm not sure what they talk about. First, it's just TV shows they both like to watch, and I'm relieved to learn, for the first time, Emily watches TV.

"Of course I watch TV, Ben!" She looks at me like "duh."

"Emily likes the same stuff I do," Elizabeth chimes in. "Reality shows: *Say Yes to the Dress, Dance Moms!*"

"Get out!" It's my only phrase I have kept up from my days in New Jersey. "And all this time I thought you only liked *Downton Abbey!*"

"I do like *Downton Abbey*," she insists. "But I like junk shows. Reality shows are like junk food. You have to let yourself go every once in a while!"

"Exactly." Elizabeth holds out her fist for a fist bump.

"Speaking of food, do you want to go get something to eat? I've got the munchies."

"Sure," Emily says, and she looks at Elizabeth. "Would you like to go?"

"No, thanks." Elizabeth gets up to go.

"Really, Elizabeth," Emily insists, "it would be nice for you to go with us. Why don't you come? It'll be fun." She has taken on a real big sister role, though I can't tell why. Maybe her own sister is too independent, too opposite her. Emily and Elizabeth have similar traits, an air of vulnerability. Still, my sister is determined not to go, which is okay with me. I don't need my little sister tagging along.

"I have homework to do, but thanks anyway." Elizabeth goes up to her room and shuts the door. Emily and I decide to head out to Adele's Corner, a kind of local Starbucks.

"I can't believe you like those garbage TV show." I back out of the garage.

"Well, I should say I used to watch them a lot." Emily folds her arms to keep herself warm as the car heats up. "Now, I have more interesting things to do." She gives me a sly look. I turn the corner onto the street that gets us out of the subdivision.

"Elizabeth sure is sweet." Emily smiles affectionately. "I wish my sister was more fun like her. My sister and I fight like cats and dogs. I guess it's because we have nothing in common. She's very athletic. But Elizabeth is a doll."

I just shake my head. Emily has a lot to learn about my family.

We get to Adele's Corner. It has a much cozier atmosphere than the big coffee chains. Adele's Corner is actually located at the corner of this little strip mall. There's a wall with large thick wooden shelves that hold books and sports memorabilia. There's also a fireplace with leather chairs next to them, and bar tables and bar chairs are along part of the glass wall, in addition to having the regular-sized tables and chairs.

She gets a Danish, along with a café mocha. I order a full lunch, ham and cheese on rye with chips and a Coke. We sit down at one of the bar tables where we can look out on the terrace where there's additional seating in warmer months. There are a couple of big-screen TVs on opposite walls. I try not to let them distract me.

"What was it like growing up with an older brother who has autism?" Emily asks out of the blue, maybe as a way to get my attention from the football game on the screen. It's a question I get asked every once in a while, or some variation of it.

"I don't know. It's all I ever knew" is my best answer. "You pretty much saw how Johnny is. He just sits there on the sofa in the sunroom and makes noises. Sometimes he rocks himself back and forth. To be honest, the noises get annoying."

Emily comes to his defense. "It seems like he was singing something. I recognize the tune a little."

"Yeah, he does that too." I pour some pepper on the sandwich I ordered, and she's still jogging her memory for the song.

"It was something like 'I can't help myself.'" The song starts forming in her mind. "La, la, la, ba, ba, ba …"

"Sugar Pie, Honey Bunch," I help out, half singing the tune. "Yeah, that's classic Johnny. He's got a whole library of those songs in his head."

"You know that I love you!" She sings the rest of the phrase and bobs her head to the beat. "That's kind of neat!" She stirs her café mocha.

"Not when he's doing it during precalculus class." I look up at the big-screen TV on the wall. "He has this period when he's supposed to be a messenger for the main office. It's at the same time I have math. We hear him all the time singing in the hallway. It's embarrassing."

"Oh, Ben." She furrows her brow and gives me that you're-a-mean-brother look.

"It's true." I tear off a piece of my sandwich. "There's this kid, Blake Barker, who's in that class. He's also on the wrestling team. I hate his guts."

"What does he do?"

"He'll make snarky remarks in class every time Johnny does his thing. When Johnny started singing that 'Moves like Jagger' song, everybody started laughing. Ms. Emerson thinks it's a hoot. She stops what she's doing and starts singing along. 'I got the moo-oo-oo-oo-ooves like Jagger!' She's not being mean or anything. It's more like she can't help herself. She gets easily distracted by things."

Emily holds her mouth to keep the café mocha she just sipped from spilling out. "That's funny!" She coughs to get the drink going down the right way. "It sounds like your teacher has attention deficit problems herself," she says after she clears her throat.

"Everybody has problems with attention!" I say rather testily. "Sorry, but it seems like everybody has that excuse."

"I'm sorry, Ben," she says softly, putting her hand on mine. "I know it must be hard sometimes. With Johnny."

"Then Blake gets up and starts dancing and singing like he's re—retarded." I normally don't have a hard time with the "R" word, but in this context, I almost get teary having that scene play in my mind.

"What a jackass!" Emily puts it succinctly. "Do they know Johnny's your brother?" I shake my head. "Ben! Why don't you tell everybody?"

"Would you tell the whole class, 'Hey, that's my brother'? It would just egg Blake on."

"Maybe not." Emily looks at me with disappointment. "Maybe other people would be a little more sensitive and tell him to knock it off."

"Would you tell everyone that he was your brother?" I get her on that point, and she presses her lips in acknowledgment.

"I'm not brave about things like that. Not like you are." She looks at me, but I just brush off her remark.

"It doesn't matter." I turn slightly in defense. "Johnny can't hear what he's saying. Even if he could, he wouldn't understand. So what difference does it make?"

"But *you* know what Blake's doing, and I think Johnny does understand a lot more than you give him credit for." Emily sounds like Mom, which makes me want to turn the subject away from Johnny and focus more on the evils of Blake.

"He's like that at wrestling too. He's a dirty wrestler. He punches, tries to poke you in the eye. This year, we're wrestling the same weight. Luckily, he wrestled with the B team that weekend you saw me. But Coach G is going to have us wrestle off to see who will be at the state tournament."

Emily lights up, as if I flipped a switch on in her head. "That should be a reality show! We'll call it *Wrestle Off!* It'll be the boys' answer to *Dance Moms!*"

"Cute!" I give her a sarcastic look.

"Seriously!" She looks out the glass wall toward the patio that has empty metal tables and chairs. "I should be a television producer. You know another idea I had for a show—your mother would like this—is tentatively titled *Take This Dog, Please!* Every week features a family that gets to pick out a dog from a local shelter. Usually they'll have some behavior problems. They have thirty days to train the dog. At the end of the show, the host asks them, 'Are you going to keep the dog? Or return the dog?'"

"But they would always keep the dog." I'm shaking my head. "Otherwise, they'll look like jerks."

"But then, there's contact info on the screen for viewers who want to rescue the dog."

"You would make a good television producer, Emily. Ironic for someone who I thought was such a bookworm."

"I am a bookworm!" She's a little indignant but confesses, "I just like the idea of being someone who can call the shots, make things happen."

I'm just glad she's got an active mind. I hear that's supposed to be the most stimulating sex organ of a woman's body. Of course, I wouldn't know that firsthand. At least not yet.

"Anyway"—she looks down, smiles shyly, and turns to look out toward the terrace—"it's just a fantasy I have!"

"Is that the only fantasy you have?" I give her a knowing smile.

"Ben!" She turns all red but grins.

"Well?" I cock my head a little.

"Let's talk about that later," she playfully chides and takes a strand of her hair and turns her head slightly. The image of that painting *The Birth of Venus* that was in one of my old history books pops into my head. That's what Emily looks like to me right now with her light reddish-brown hair and her triangular face looking so delicate. All she needs is to be naked. Just like Venus.

Chapter 16

We have one more tournament, the Northern Virginia Invitational, to go to before gearing up for the state championship. It's held at this high school about a half hour east of North Central High. It will be the second match Emily agrees to go to, and I appreciate her willingness to come. I know for the most part wrestling isn't a sport a lot of girls can get into. Even my own mother has a hard time getting into it.

Around eleven o'clock, I see Emily stepping up into the bleachers. She looks sad, like something happened before she got to the gym. I know this sounds bad, but this is not how I want the guys to see my new girlfriend. I want them to see the swan she's turned into. I want them to see how happy she is, now that she is with me. But all she is doing is looking intently at her cell phone. I've never seen her playing games on her phone before. This is weird. Something is wrong.

I go up the bleacher seats and sit next to her.

"Hi." I try to sound upbeat.

"Hi," she says flatly.

"Everything okay?"

"Yeah, everything's okay. Have you played yet?"

"No, I haven't wrestled yet."

She still hasn't looked up. "Good. I'm glad I didn't miss you."

"Emily, is something wrong?" Now I'm starting to get really worried that she wants to break up with me. That's a fear I always have in the back of my mind. But then, if she wants to break up with me, why would she come to my match? This back-and-forth goes on in my head any time she says she can't go somewhere with me.

"I'm okay." She smiles bravely at me.

"Wish me luck." I look at her, trying to make eye contact.

"Good luck, Ben!" She finally looks at me and gives me a closed-mouth smile. I reach over to kiss her. I'm hoping the guys see us, so I try to hold her a little longer.

"Ben, you are kind of sweaty." She backs off a bit.

"Sorry." I'm still feeling uneasy as I head back down toward the mat. I have to shake it off and get my head into wrestling mode.

I get on the mat and wrestle with this kid from Robbinsville, one of the top schools in the region. We both score two points for an escape. It's not until the last twenty seconds that I manage to get a takedown.

I look at Emily as the referee holds up my arm. She's smiling, and I smile bigger than I've done since I've wrestled at North Central.

I get to the table. They tell me I won't be having another match for another hour. That's the way wrestling tournaments usually go.

So I go up to the bleachers and suggest we go get lunch. She smiles sadly and takes my hand, and we step down and head to the cafeteria. I buy three slices of pizza and two drinks.

"Dad's got orders, Ben," she tells me bluntly after we get settled. "We're moving to North Carolina in January!"

I feel like she just punched me in the gut and all the wind is knocked out of me. I put my slice of pizza back down on the paper plate. "But you said you were here to stay for at least two years!

"That's what the plan was," she said with a quivering voice and crumbles up her napkin. "I don't know what's going on. Dad won't say much. I hear everything through Mom. She's angry, but she's a marine wife. You learn to shrug it off and start packing up."

"Can't you stay here until the end of the year?"

"That's not the way it works, Ben. Especially with my father. When it's time to move out, we move out."

It feels like she is rejecting me. Although rationally I know that isn't the case, that's how it feels.

"I'm sorry, Ben. It appears that something happened at the base in North Carolina, and they need someone quick to take over."

"What happened? Did someone go nuts and do something?" I don't know much about what goes on at these military bases. The only thing I can think of is Fort Hood. She hunches her shoulders forward, giving me the real scoop.

"It seems like the colonel was caught having an affair with another officer's wife," she says, infuriated.

"So?" I dismiss the story right out of hand. "That stuff happens all the time in Washington! Did he take a selfie or something?"

"The guy isn't that stupid, Ben!" Emily gets irritated at my ignorance about military protocol, or whatever it is. "They thought they had everything kept hush-hush, but it sooner or later comes out. At least that's what Daddy says. When this happens, your career is over. So my father has to go there and take over command."

"Great!" I slap my hand on the chair arm. "This old fart can't keep his hands to himself, and I get punished for it!" I give Emily an angry expression, like it's her fault. "An old geezer has one woman plus another on the side, and I get nothing!"

"Ben!" It's her turn to get mad at me.

"I'm sorry!" I apologize for my outburst, but she should apologize for not going further than just making out in the car. Then I ask her a painful what-if question. "Do you think it would happen if you could stay here?"

Emily looks down and doesn't answer for a few seconds. "I don't know, Ben. You know, I'm old-fashioned about all that. If we just had a little more time. We can still keep in touch."

"Yeah, I guess so. It's so unfair." I'm saying what's in my heart, laying my thoughts out there. "I know there's nothing you can do, but I can't help thinking, 'Why?' Things were going so well. At least they were for me."

"I'm thinking the same thing, Ben." She's in tears now. I'm starting to well up myself. "I hate my father's life sometimes."

"Well, it's not his fault," I say.

"I know that, but I tell you what"—she shakes her head, staring off into the distance—"I never want to move again! I've had it. Mom always tells me how lucky we are to have been to so many places while most people just live their whole lives in one place. 'It's so enriching!' she says. She grew up in a small town, so she likes it, or at least, she doesn't mind it. She even keeps a lot of boxes still packed! My sister is okay with it. It's just another move to her, but then she's in seventh grade."

I sit silently, still ticked off with this creep who has screwed my life. "Was it really worth it?" I want to ask him, this faceless old man whom I can't help but picture with his pants down. That makes me even more furious.

"This isn't supposed to happen." She gets more animated. "We were supposed to stay here! Finish here! Why is it that when something good happens to me, I get yanked away?"

"You'll still see me while you're still here, won't you?" I look at her as if my life depends on her answer.

She returns my gaze with sad but hopeful eyes. "Of course, Ben!" She looks down at the table. "I'm so unsure about everything, though. I just wish we had more time together. We still have our books! By the way, did you ever start reading *The Old Man and the Sea*?"

"No, and I don't think I want to read about any old men right now." I bite off part of the crust of the pizza, wishing it is that old fart's head.

Emily shrugs. "Well, you pick out a book for us to read. Some classic."

"I'm thinking I want to read an alternative history book," I say sorely. "That's what I want for us."

Chapter 17

The winter of my discontent begins as I say good-bye to Emily. We say our last absolute good-bye at Sergeants Restaurant, where we had our first date. It's lunchtime, so we order sandwiches and chips. She's leaving for North Carolina right after.

I drop her off at her house and walk her to her waiting car. The house is empty. Her mother and sister say hello to me briefly as they head back into the house to give it one last check. She tells me again that she will stay in touch with me forever.

"Do you really mean that?" I take her in my arms and hold her tight.

"Ben!" She gasps, and I release her a little.

"Sorry, I just don't want to let you go," I say as I try to not get too emotional.

"Yes." She leans back and looks at me. "I want to leave you with a phrase I love."

"Oh, you have some phrases you actually love?" I laugh teasingly.

"Yeah, not many." She laughs and then whispers, "But here's one: 'Love never fails.' I know it's not original, but it's true. And no matter what happens, Ben, believe it."

I tell her sister and mother to have a safe trip, and I head back to my car, totally drained. The idea that she'll fade away from my life has been a constant source of anxiety for me these last couple weeks. Brian's already gone. I haven't heard from Seth since the beginning of school. That's just the way it is.

"I hate that phrase," Emily would say. It's on her list of hated phrases, but it's true. People come and go. That's just the way it is. It's just a matter of time before I'm nothing more than a memory.

My life begins a downward spiral of depression, like I am in a dark dank well that I can't climb out of. I don't care about anything. I just go through the motions. Elizabeth and I make snide remarks to each other. My mother yells at me to clean up around the house more, and I yell back at my mother.

"Take the garbage out, Benjamin," she calls down into the basement.

"Okay, I'll do it in a minute," I tell her as I am working out math problems.

"Do it now!" she insists.

"I have to do my homework!" I yell at her.

"Just take out the garbage, and then you can do your homework." She raises her voice. "Why can't you just do what I ask you—"

"Damn it, I will!"

Dad, who's been sitting in his recliner watching television in the basement, comes to my rescue. "Diane, he'll get the garbage later."

The sound of a door slamming emanates from the top of the basement stairs. "I'll just do it myself."

She always likes playing the martyr.

Wrestling season is a dark time anyway, literally. It happens over the course of December, January, and February. It makes sense because it's an inside sport. I used to love it, though. I loved challenging myself, which wrestling provides in a way that baseball, football, and basketball cannot. You can never blame anyone else for something going wrong if you lose. If you lose, it's because the other guy was better and he won or you were not thinking or lazy and didn't practice.

That's what the wrestle-off would prove. Mike Duhon got bumped up this season to a higher weight. The other guy on the team who was at that same weight didn't have a chance.

"Hey, Mike," this kid named Pete says half-jokingly, "why didn't you just pin me, put me out of my misery quickly?"

"I like to play with my food before I devour it!" Mike says with a smile, wiping the pretend sweat off his arms. I wish things were that easy in my weight bracket, where most high school wrestlers tend to converge. Mike always seems to be above it all in every way possible. He's got the looks and the athleticism and the confidence that naturally come with having it all. I quickly put my jealousy out of my mind; otherwise I'd literally go out of my mind.

So I turn off my mind, get on my phone, and play games. I barely have the capacity to concentrate on school. Coach G doesn't intimidate me anymore. Nothing much excites me.

"Hey, you okay?" J. T. nudges my arm. "You look real sad. Like somebody died."

We sit there letting the wall of the gym hold up our backs. I hesitate before I answer. Will I be able to put back all those sad feelings once I let them out? I decide to tell J. T. anyway. "My girlfriend moved away."

"You had a girlfriend?" J. T. asks, almost shocked.

"I met her at your party, the one you had at the beginning of the school year."

"Oh." He smiles. "Wow. Yeah, now I remember. She was that girl I saw you with at Robbinsville. Good-looking girl, Ben. Didn't realize it was serious."

"Yeah, she goes to Adele High." I feel good that J. T. saw me with her and called her good-looking, as though I am validated as being an eligible romantic interest.

"Oh, well, sorry to hear that," J. T. mutters. Then he puts his chin in his hand and thinks, or does the closest thing J. T. does to thinking deeply. "Well, that's too bad, Ben." He pauses and pokes my bicep. "But I learned something today. It's better to have loved and lost than to have never loved at all. That's from a poet, Lord Tennyson," he tells me, as though he's trying to impress me. "So it's true."

"Yeah," I say, thinking it's nice that J. T. can quote poets besides Kanye West. "Maybe that's right. It still hurts, though."

"I'm glad I can love so many." He nods his head, looking uncharacteristically philosophical. "You know, Ben, the more you love, the less it hurts."

"How's that?" I open up my bottled water and take a swig.

"It just gets easier to dump a girl the more you do it." He folds his arms, as if he's given the matter full consideration and is satisfied with his conclusion.

"I wish I had as many girls as you, J. T.," I say. "But I don't know how I could take so many breakups. Especially if they are at the same school."

"Good thing North Central is a big school," he says. "Plus, I go knowing they enjoyed it as much as I did."

"Enjoyed?" I look at him askance.

"The love," J. T. says, "the love. It felt good to both of us."

"Are you talking about sex?" I am trying not to sound like a prude. But he probably already thinks that way about me anyway. I am no Mike Duhon.

"Sex and love, Ben," J. T. insists. "For me, sex is love."

"But you go to church." I know that doesn't always correlate to sexual purity, but with J. T., I've never thought of him being a hard-core lothario. (*That's from Shakespeare, J. T. He was a poet too!*) J. T. is just so innocent-looking. Plus, I really thought he took

135

his religion seriously. "Don't you feel bad that you are committing fornication?"

"Hey, Ben, I'm not into *that*!" J. T. sounds disgusted.

"J. T., it means you're having sex outside of marriage," I tell him. "Jesus spoke against it."

"When?" He looks at me skeptically. "When did Jesus say anything about that?"

"In the Gospels," I answer. "He warned against sexual immorality."

"Oh!" J. T. snorts and breathes a sigh of relief. "That's different! Don't worry, Ben. I wouldn't read too much into that." He takes a swig of water from his bottle and turns his attention to the mat.

"No, J. T."—I shake my head—"I guess you wouldn't."

But J. T., by musing on the wisdom of Lord Tennyson, gets me thinking. Maybe it is better to not have a conscience and have sex anyway, better to not worry if the girl gets pregnant or has some STD. Why worry whether her parents care if she does or doesn't? And what if she turns into an obsessed person who stalks you or openly accuses you of raping her? I think about those things. Whether it comes from my upbringing or my innate hesitancy, I don't know. I just know I feel a sense of guilt about things that are only in my fantasies.

Chapter 18

Winters in Adele are like everything else about this dumb town. Annoying. For the past two years, we have had record snow, but the county or city managers, or whoever it is who calls out the snowplows, act as if it's the first time so much snow has been dumped on us. So the first day of every snow dump, it's like the whole town stops and stands like a bunch of dodo birds. School starts two hours later and throws everything off.

It's a far cry from Fargo. There's a reason they put the national wrestling championships in Fargo, North Dakota—as a test of endurance. That's what winters in other places do—they give people a chance to put their survival skills to the test. Here in Adele, it's just a time to get depressed.

I really don't care about states anymore, but I have to. Dad is expecting me to wrestle. Blake and I have been alternating going to different tournaments throughout the season. Coach G says we're about even. If I wasn't so depressed and actually cared, I think I could beat Blake easily, no problem. But I can't shake off this pervasive aura of hopelessness surrounding me.

Mom says I need to get out more. "Take the dog out for a walk. There's nothing like taking a walk to clear the head." I snap at her a lot because it gets me going, to be honest. I have to get mad, because if I don't get mad, I won't get up in the morning. So every morning it's the same thing.

"Benjamin, hurry up, we'll be late for school!" she yells from downstairs.

"I'm getting ready, damn it!"

"Don't you use talk like that with me!" Mom screams back.

"Why do you have to get so mad, Benjamin?" Elizabeth chimes in. "I can't stand it!"

"Then move out!" I yell at her as I run down the stairs into the kitchen

"Don't tell her what to do!" Mom greets me at the landing. "This isn't your house!"

"No," I say in the most hateful way I can, "and I can't wait to get out of this damn house. You were never a mother to me anyway. Just to Elizabeth and Johnny."

Mom's lips quiver. "Get in the car." She turns and walks toward the garage.

This is negative motivation—at least that's what I call it. It may be unpleasant, but positive thinking is beyond me right now, so being angry is the only way I know how to deal with life. It's the only thing I can grasp. This afternoon, I will wrestle Blake for the position at states. I have to get "the fire in the belly," even if it gives everyone else an ulcer.

I'm sleepwalking throughout the day. But I'm still ready for Blake. We get on the mat. I know what Blake does on the mat; all his moves are fairly predictable after watching him for two-plus years. So I'm able to counter every one of his moves. I just need to make a decisive move.

What's so annoying is that he keeps running off the mat. But in the third round, I won't let him go. I'm about to go for his legs when I feel a right hook coming up and knocking the left side of my jaw. I fall to the floor, a little dazed. That's when he grabs me by the waist and throws me down for a pin.

The assistant coach slaps the mat, indicating a pin.

Didn't he see Blake punch me? I'm thinking to myself. I get up and look at Blake, who's walking off the mat with a smug look on his face. I look around the room for a witness. By J. T.'s and Mike's expressions, I can tell they saw something. But they just stand there, as if they're in a daze themselves.

I can almost read their minds. *"Don't say anything to Coach G. Don't want to rock the boat. Just let it be."* All I want to do is scream, *"It's not fair! You all saw what Blake did. He cheated! Somebody say something!"* But we are all shocked, speechless. At least I am.

I turn to look for Coach G's reaction. He's talking to the assistant coach. I'm hoping he'll tell Coach G about the punch. But all Coach G says is "Wow, I wasn't expecting that, Blake. Good job."

Chapter 19

It's already April, and wrestling season is over but the winter season is still going on this year. It matches my mood. The only good thing that came out of wrestling was that Blake got disqualified for unsportsmanlike conduct on the mat. It's bittersweet justice.

I go to the second-tier tournaments. At least I win being a big fish in a small ponds. The nice thing about going to these matches is that everyone isn't so eaten up by winning. The schools are smaller, some of them are private schools, and I get to talk to some of the guys at All Saints, this Christian school that has a pretty good team. Even their coach comes up to me and congratulates me.

"You've got a lot of talent," he tells me after I pin one of his wrestlers. It feels good to get a little recognition every once in a while. I wish I got more from Emily these days.

When she left in mid-January, she sent me texts almost right away. Even though she said her parents limited her phone and tablet use, she would still send me e-mails. "I'm supposed to be doing my homework now, so I can't be long. Miss you much!" Then she would put a heart symbol at the end.

I have to admit, my messages sounded angry at times. "Why haven't you texted back?! I left you a message at your home number. Did you get it?" At first, she would just respond with "Relax, Ben! I can't jump every time you say jump!" I would go back and apologize. Long-distance relationships are no fun.

The only creature who's excited by the snow is Rosie. Something about the cold air makes her bounce from room to room and slide to the door, begging to get out and play in the snow.

"Come on, Momma, Ah want to play in the snow!"

"Okay, Rosie." Mom rubs the mutt's face. "As soon as I take everyone to school. You want to hop in the car?" I hate it that Mom has to drive us to school. "You could all take the bus!" she reminds me in her nagging voice. But that's a worse option. The ideal option would be for me to have a car of my own and get a student parking permit. Too bad Dad sold the Chevy Tahoe.

Elizabeth has dance practice after school at Rosemary Butler's School of Dance, where all the girls on the dance team go during their off-season. I have practice until six, sometimes later, so I'm reasonable enough to see that it doesn't work out logistically. But to be honest, I don't know which is worse, being seen getting out of the car with Johnny, where everyone at the school drop-off can see him galloping with his arms flapping about, or being the only junior still riding the school bus.

Mom loves the fact that she has all of her children going to the same school, "finally!" She gets a big kick out of taking us to school, pretending that we are all one big happy family. She takes Rosie along for the ride (*"Ah have to protect mah human puppies when they go to school!"*). The dog-in-the-car routine has gotten old. It may be cute up to about middle school, but it's irritating when she barks at every motorcycle and every school bus that passes by.

"Shut up, Rosie!" I rest my elbow on the door and put my head in my hand.

"She's just looking out for you, Benjamin!" Mom chides.

"The girls on the dance team think she's cute," Elizabeth opines. *Well, thank God for that!*

I switch the radio station from the Christian music to one of the local stations playing alternative music, or at least some palatable pop songs.

"Turn it to B-100," Elizabeth orders. "They're going to be broadcasting today at Rosemary Butler's. I want to hear them make an announcement." Mom takes over the knob and sets it on 100.1, the pop station "broadcasting out of Leesburg throughout the DC area," with the most insipid DJs, Jay and Britney. Sure enough, being ever the cheerleader that she is for the station, Britney gives a teaser.

"Be sure to keep it on B-100 this afternoon for the craziest dance girls *evah!*" Britney says in that gushing tone that is her trademark. "I'm talking about what everyone is talking about, this dance team right out of Adele that has been quite a sensation on all the social media!"

"Yeah, those girls are a talented group, aren't they?" Jay says in a creepy way, or maybe it just sounds creepy to me. "I saw their YouTube video—"

"Uh-huh," Britney interjects.

"And, let me tell you, these girls are hot! Am I allowed to say that?" Jay asks.

"Well, let me put it this way. I wish I could do those moves!" Britney laughs in a suggestive way.

I look over at Mom, who has her shoulders hunched up and a look of alarm frozen on her face. "What are they talking about?" She looks into the rearview mirror at Elizabeth.

"We're just doing this dance routine," Elizabeth says dismissively. "It's nothing."

"Why haven't I seen it?" Mom's voice starts rising. Fortunately for Elizabeth, we are about to approach the drop-off circle, which means we have to prepare Johnny, who is slow about disembarking from the car. Johnny gets obsessed with making sure he wipes off his seat and pulling the seat belt strap until it catches in its locked position, not letting the buckle dangle on the car floor.

"Come on, Johnny," Elizabeth orders. "Move it! It's okay, your seat is fine! You don't have to brush it," she rushes him. "The seat belt is okay." We take turns every week sitting in the back with him, doing Johnny duty.

"Have a good day." Mom's voice has a little edge to it. I predict the first thing she will do when she gets home, before she even walks the dog, is check out the video.

Sure enough, I get home and Mom and Dad are sitting on the sofa with the television off, and Elizabeth is sitting in the chair in the corner facing them. It's just a chair to take up space. No one sits there unless company comes over—or someone is in trouble and needs straightening out.

"Benjamin?" Dad asks. "Have you seen this video the dance team made?"

My mind scrambles around to get into spin mode. I don't want Elizabeth to get into trouble, but the truth is I've seen the video; it's the talk of Twitter and everywhere else. "It's like those dances on that show *Dance Moms*. It's no big deal." I shrug.

"Some of those dances they have those girls do are pretty risqué," Mom counters. "This is beyond that."

"Oh, Mom! It's no big deal!" I yell.

"We'll decide that, Benjamin," Dad jumps in.

Elizabeth shouts her case. "Mom, you've seen us at the games! You know the moves. You've seen us shake our butts!"

"But I've *never* seen you spank yourselves!" She shakes her head slowly and folds her arms.

"Miss Rosemary said we just needed to do that to get a reaction. Create some buzz!"

"We're buzzing, all right!" Dad looks like he's about to bite someone's head off. "Can you believe this, Diane? Do the other parents just let their daughters dance—I won't even call it dancing! Why not just get out the pole!"

"There is a pole dancing class offered at Rosemary's," Mom says almost under her breath. "Tuesday mornings." She looks at Dad. Dad's expression changes from one of disgust to one of amusing consideration back to looking disgusted when he notices I'm looking at him.

"And you let our daughter take dance there?" Dad asks indignantly.

"She's the best in the business, Keith!"

"I don't want our daughter in that kind of business!" Dad's whole face is tightening up. He leans over to Mom, trying to keep his voice down but fails, as usual. "Maybe we should call her Madam Rosemary!"

"Oh, Dad!" Elizabeth shouts.

I sit on the end of the sofa and add my support to Elizabeth. "It's just the way people dance these days. Jeez!"

Rosemary Butler may have been quite a dancer twenty-five years ago, but she's long in the tooth. She's got long thin legs holding up a sagging middle section. Not that I try to study her looks too much. I mean, that's a little gross, but I have to say her butt looks weird. It's like she has no butt at all—just thin legs and a big middle, and the long bleached blonde hair is doing her leathery-looking face no favors.

Dad has made up his mind. "We need to talk to Madam Rosemary, Elizabeth."

"Oh my God!" Elizabeth springs out of the chair. "You are making the video into a big deal, and it is *nothing*! Why don't you mind your own business?" She doesn't wait for the answer and runs up to her room, where Dad would probably have sent her anyway.

I follow her up, figuring I can try to calm her down. I tiptoe up to her door and listen to her talking to herself in between crying and sniffling. "I can't help it if I'm better than they are! They're just a bunch of jealous bit—"

I knock on her door and ask if I can come in. There is dead silence before she gives a faint yes. I enter her room of over-the-top girlie-ness. Elizabeth's room is decorated with dance posters hung on pale purple walls. She has a big four-poster white-painted bed with pink and white bedcovers and pillows. Mom painted a picture of her in a tutu when she was about eight that still hangs over her bed. I don't enter in here often, so I tread cautiously to the foot of the bed and sit halfway on the mattress.

She's lying faceup on her bed, looking like a cadaver with her eyes staring at the ceiling. She pierces the morbid silence with a whine. "Why do they have to make a big deal of the video?" *Sniff, sniff, hiccup.* "That's not even the big issue I'm having with the dance team!"

I feel a groundswell of emotions coming on, so I try to placate her. "What's going on?" I sit at the corner of the bed, trying to sound like a shrink.

"Well"—she takes in a deep breath—"Heather sends a text to Millie and Skylar. She goes, 'Who does this Lizzie McDowell think she is? Awfully bossy for a freshman!' And then Millie goes, 'I know, thinks she does the routine better than everyone else!' Then Skylar goes, 'She's Miss Rosemary's favorite.'" Elizabeth wipes her nose with her arm and continues, "Then Heather says, 'Know what my mom calls her? Rosemary's baby!'" Elizabeth burst out crying all over again.

"And somehow this all gets back to you?" I nod, trying to look sympathetic.

She lets out shallow breaths and nods. "Now that's all I get at practice: 'There goes Rosemary's baby!' 'Look at Rosemary's baby!'" A new wave of tears comes over her face. I wait for her to calm down.

"So?" I ask calmly.

She bolts up like I just sent her a shock of electricity through her body. She gnashes her teeth, and her eyes look like they could come out of their sockets.

"So?" she hisses at me. "Is that all you can say? I'm being treated like a pariah and you say *'so'!*"

"Just don't let it get to you." I speak slowly, trying to calm her down.

"You don't get anything, do you?" She huffs. "Get out, Benjamin. I need my space!"

She throws herself over on her stomach and wallows in the drama that is the dance team. I am all too happy to honor her request. I meet Mom in the upstairs hallway as I come out of Elizabeth's room.

"I can't wait to get away from here!" I mutter under my breath. Mom looks at me with curiosity and takes a pause before knocking on Elizabeth's door.

On Monday, things take a serious turn when Heather posts a picture on her Instagram of Elizabeth on the bull's-eye of a target. "The person on the bull's-eye is there because she better watch out! Elizabeth, you are so full of yourself. You think you are the best dancer on the team. Well, honey, I think you need to be a little less cocky!"

It's actually so dumb, but Elizabeth takes it too seriously. "I'm thinking now is a good time for Dad and Mom to say something to someone!" she says as we sit on a bench, waiting for Mom to come pick us up after our practices. "Either Miss Rosemary or the principal. This is cyberbullying!"

"Come on, Elizabeth, she doesn't mean what she's saying!" I just don't want this to escalate. I hate attention, especially bad attention caused by one of my siblings.

"Then why is she saying it?" Elizabeth screams at me. "She's just jealous that I'm better than she is. I can't help that." She gets herself all worked up, starting with the wobbly voice and then the sniffles. "I'm not trying to brag. I don't brag at all. I just do my work. I start taking dance seriously, and where does it get me? On a target!" She throws herself into her arms and falls into her lap.

"You're not going to tell Mom and Dad, are you?"

"Why shouldn't I? I'm not a victim, Benjamin! I'm not taking this lying down!" She goes back to burying her face in her arms.

I put up with Blake all the time. If I said something, I'd be an outcast on the team. On the other hand, if I could do what I wanted to do, which is to punch him out cold, I'd be suspended. It must be nice being a girl, being able to tattle. But then, that's what Elizabeth has always done best.

The next day, our father calls the principal at North Central and demands to meet with him that day. "Your father was telling that secretary of his that if he didn't make time today, your father would be contacting our attorney." Mom gives me an update as she is driving with me to the store to get some extra protein bars. For some reason, it's easier for me to talk to her in the car, even with that mutt barking in the background.

"I don't mean to sound nonchalant," I say, sounding as nonchalant as possible, "but don't you think you and Dad are taking this a little too seriously? I mean, this stuff happens all the time."

"Oh, really?" Mom gives me that tone that says she doesn't want any excuses. "Well, this is wrong, Benjamin. It doesn't happen to the McDowell family." Great, this is one more thing my mother has to get worked up about. Usually, it's about Johnny and whether he's getting all the help he needs and all that stuff. But since he's practically an adult, I think she realizes how hopeless he is, even though she won't say it.

"*What a bunch of nasty girls!*" Rosie says. It's ironic that Rosie, of all creatures, won't use the "B" word.

"Mom, girls talk like this about each other all the time. It's human nature."

"Exactly, Benjamin! This is the way people normally act. Like a bunch of animals." This is going to be a long car ride. I feel a life lesson talk coming on. "It's not normal to show restraint, to keep your mouth shut when someone attacks you any more than it is natural to shave and put on deodorant. But we do that to show we're civilized. We're young gentlemen and ladies."

"I wish you could tell this to Blake Barker," I say with tension throughout my face. "He makes fun of Johnny's singing all the time."

Mom's forehead wrinkles. "When does he do this?" Funny how when it's about Johnny, she starts showing concern.

"In precalc class, I thought I told you. He imitates Johnny's singing." I go back and explain to her about how we hear Johnny out in the hallway for his office helper class and how Blake responds with a mean comment."

"I don't remember you telling me this." She shakes her head slightly. Her voice starts to raise slightly. "Does the teacher do anything?"

"Yeah, somebody'll say something to him like 'Shut up' or 'That's mean.' It's really no big deal." I realize I need to walk this back or else she'll have something else to complain about to the principal. I want to make the point that I am being a gentleman. I am showing restraint. I want to punch Blake out. But I'm a gentleman. Not that it's gotten me anywhere. But I drop it.

Mom is tapping her fingers on the steering wheel, like she is trying to come up with something constructive to say. "Well," she says finally, "if he ever tries anything again, you just wait until after school to punch him back. You can't get in trouble then."

"That's showing violence, Mom," I tell her, just giving the facts. "That's not being a gentleman."

"There's a time to fight and a time for peace." Mom does her go-to thing and quotes the Bible. "It's all in the timing, Benjamin."

"Sure, Mom." I turn the radio up and switch to my station.

Chapter 20

I'm doing my homework at the kitchen table when I hear Mom, Dad, and Elizabeth come in from the garage. Mom gives a look of triumph as she walks in and throws her purse on the island counter. Elizabeth is beaming.

Thanks to Mom and Dad's intervention, the entire dance team will go through a group therapy session, where they will have a "talk out" to air out their feelings in a "safe, all-affirming, and nurturing environment."

"Do your impression of Miss Rosemary!" Elizabeth eggs on Mom to perform.

"Do it, Diane." Dad laughs. "Do your interpretive dance routine!"

Mom starts posing like Miss Rosemary, with her hands on her hips, flicking her long hair off her shoulders. "I want you all to talk with your bodies!" Mom says with the voice of the gravelly teacher. She starts throwing her arms and legs out in dramatic style. "Show me what you are saying with your arms, your legs, your torso! Girls, if you could talk with your bodies as well as you blabber with your mouths, you'd be phenomenal! We'd have our own television show!"

Elizabeth squeals at that last line. The thought of being on television leaves her speechless. "The girls are all excited." Mom smiles proudly at Elizabeth and gives her a hug. "I'm so proud of you, sweetheart!"

"Thanks, Mom," Elizabeth says.

To keep up the newfound goodwill (and to keep the dance team from getting sidelined next year, according to Dad), Dr. Hemphill, the principal at North Central, suggests to all dance families that they take a brief hiatus from all online activities that don't involve schoolwork. Cell phones are taken away "indefinitely" until the students learn to say positive things about each other.

In the McDowell family, this means everyone, including Elizabeth and me, has their cell phone privileges revoked. So I can't text Emily anymore, and the computer in the study is off-limits since it is in a closed room where it can't be monitored.

"Why do I have to get punished?" I protest. "How am I going to contact Emily?"

"Try writing a letter." Mom smiles.

"You're kidding!" I am so angry right now.

"Love takes effort, Ben!" She's loving this ban, and so does Dad. "We can finally have some family time, get us talking to each other," he enthuses. "We'll play games after supper together, like Catch Phrase!"

Wow, what fun! I can't wait. "At least let me e-mail Emily and tell her I will be unreachable for the next week."

"I think it's actually a good thing," Emily tells me on Skype. "My parents are really strict about us using tablets. We're not allowed to have them in our bedrooms. That means we have to read, Ben!" She grins.

"Well, it's not fair!" Her attitude is not making me any less angry. In fact, I'm a little miffed that she isn't upset that this means we can't talk to each other for a long time.

"Life isn't fair, Ben." She rolls her eyes. "I hate that phrase. I've heard it so many times, but it's true!"

I am about to ask her about how things are in North Carolina when she tells me that she has to go. "See, Ben? I have limits on my Internet use too."

"I never realized that before," I tell her, and she just says it's because we've spent so much time talking about how we won't be able to talk to each other.

"I guess you can write me," she says.

"Sure," I say with no enthusiasm. "That's what my mother told me to do."

"Well, you can try it if you want to," she says with resignation. I guess I'm starting to sound like a whiner, so I work up some enthusiasm for the idea.

"That's what I'm gonna do." I sound overly chipper. "Expect a letter in the mail in a few days."

"Okay, Ben. Well, gotta go."

Perhaps this will be a good experiment, writing a letter on paper. I don't write on paper except for taking notes in class. The only person I ever write letters to is my grandmother to thank her for a birthday gift or Christmas gift. Those letters consist of usually no more than three sentences.

This letter to Emily has to be big, like one of those lost letters historians find that shows the true feelings of some famous person, which disputes the common perception that said famous person was a cold, unemotional person. I'm lying in bed, staring at the ceiling, with a textbook for a desk and a blank piece of paper waiting to hold all my feelings for her.

"Dear Emily," I write down. That's the usual beginning, not so hard. It's what to put down after that's racking my brain. I don't want to get too mushy, but I want to show her my true feelings, give her something in writing that she can frame in her heart. Wow. That actually sounds romantic.

Dear Emily,

No text or email could convey the deep feelings I have for you. With my not-so-great, yet sincere penmanship, I want to tell you my true feelings and deep love for you that you can hold inside your heart.

I read it over and over again. I stare at the paper, as if, like in that Harry Potter book, someone else's writing will magically appear in response. I want a response right now, to tell me to go on, to keep writing. But there's nothing, so I plow ahead.

I miss you so much even though you are in my thoughts constantly. If only I could live on that, but I miss your presence, your smell, your smile, your warm body next to mine. I miss your kisses, your touch. I can't wait for spring break, when I can go down and see you. I just need that little time together to be able to make it through the rest of the year.

You mean so much to me, Emily. I hope you don't hate that phrase. It sounds so trite. But it's true. I love you. I can't wait to see you. I'm glad I have written this letter. It has been good to my soul to write out my feelings. Now that they're on paper, the feelings of anguish, of not being able to see you, are easier to bear, if that makes sense.

Good night, Em. See you soon. Love, Ben.

It isn't Shakespeare, but it is the best I can do in an hour when it's getting after midnight. I fold the typing paper up in three sections. I'll get an envelope in the morning.

It is weeks before I get a letter back from her. Mom tells me in the car on the way back home from school that I got a letter. It's the brightest spot to a really good day. I got two exams back, a B+ in precalc, and an A– in history. Both were the highest in the class. On top of that, I have no wrestling practice, which was getting to be a pain, even in the off-season when it isn't so intense.

I take the letter up to my room. It is a business-sized envelope with a North Carolina return address with only her last name. It isn't very romantic-looking, but then neither was mine. My heart starts pounding in excitement. I sit on my bed, staring at it for a few moments before opening it up. It feels different getting something that I know she touched.

As carefully as I can, I tear it open and pull out her letter. It is written on copying paper too.

Dear Ben,

Writing a letter sure isn't as easy as I thought it would be. I thought being the reader that I am, I could come up with some clever lines. But oh well, here goes.

Ben, as I settle into my new high school, I realize that our high school years are a time for growth, a time to move forward. It is a time to experience new things and test our inner strength. It's time we both lived in the now, and that's hard to do when your mind is one place and your body is in another. So as hard as it is, we must move on from each other.

I just want to thank you, Ben, for believing in me, for making me feel so beautiful. You are a wonderful guy, Ben. You're bright and handsome. You really are. The girl who ends up with you is one lucky girl.

I hated writing this letter, Ben. I hate that I used so many trite, worn-out phrases, but most of all, I hate it because I know it is going to hurt you. I am so sorry. But we both know it's for the best. I will always love you and think about you. You are a very special person, Ben. Please know that.

Love, Emily

My mouth and eyes start watering. Now I wish I could throw up. But I just sit there on my bed, slightly shaking involuntarily. I take a deep breath, trying not to give in, but I can't help it. I start sobbing. I cry for a few minutes and then realize I can't stand being in my room. I need to get out, to move. So I put on some running shorts and a T-shirt and go out for a run.

I have been around enough military families to know that long distance doesn't kill relationships. I know what Emily meant when she talked about moving on. She found someone else. I'm just surprised at how quickly she dropped me. But I'm not surprised that someone else fell for her. She's a beauty, and now she knows it. I should have known I couldn't keep that fact from her.

I'm going to run until my legs give out. Then I'll run some more.

I make a decision not to wallow in self-pity. I can't. If I let it get to me, I don't know what I might do. I have to crawl out of this hole and fast. I get home and find my phone in the pocket of the jeans I wore to school. I send a text: "Pls destroy my letter. Text me to let me know when it's done."

She texts me back within fifteen minutes with a simple "Done." Amazing how she doesn't put up a fight, doesn't even feign one, suggesting that we still keep in touch. That cuts me even deeper. I immediately delete her number from my phone. I go into my e-mail account, phone contacts, Twitter, and Facebook, deleting all vestiges of her. Emily will be relegated to memory status. She is to be known as my first kiss, my first love, much in the same way Brian is known as my first best friend but is no more to me than that. Come to think of it, I suppose that kid Travis in Oakwood would be considered my first best friend. I forgot about him. But that's the idea.

I just want to go for a drive now, so I run downstairs and see Mom fixing dinner. She gives me a sad, pained look, as if she knows what's going on. "Can I go get you something from the store?" That's usually how I tell her I need to go for a drive.

"I could use some French bread." She smiles with her mouth, but her eyes are full of pity. "We're having spaghetti tonight." Dad usually has red wine with spaghetti. I could use some.

I don't want to be alone in the car, but then I don't want to talk to anyone either. Having Johnny in the car, I can have both of those options. I go over to the sunroom where Johnny is sitting with his earphones plugged into his iPod. I tap him on the knee and pull one earbud out of his ear. "Johnny, want to go to the store?"

"Yes." Going to the store is one of his favorite things to do. Even he needs to get off the couch every once in a while. He immediately gets up to go out.

As soon as we are headed out of the driveway, I turn on the radio and Johnny starts rocking back and forth. It's his way of dancing to the music, but it bothers me. "Johnny, stop rocking." He keeps on rocking until I turn off the radio.

"Let's just talk, Johnny," I say to keep my thoughts away from my pain. I start asking him questions he knows the answers to. There are lots of these rote questions Mom has taught Johnny.

155

"How was school today?"

"School was fun," he answers robotically.

"We're having spaghetti tonight. Do you like spaghetti?"

"Yes."

"What other foods do you like?"

"Spaghetti."

"Yes, Johnny, you like spaghetti, and what other foods do you like to eat?" I prompt again.

"Pizza, hamburger, and chicken nuggets."

"That's good." I give up on the conversation. I just don't have the patience Mom has in having the same conversation over and over. So I start talking to him, telling Johnny things I want to say but can't say to anyone else. "It's good that you don't like people touching you, Johnny. You don't want people touching you."

"No touch." He sounds like a male version of Siri.

"That's right, no touch," I tell him.

Johnny starts rocking back and forth again. "Boy, you're gonna carry that weight, carry that weight, carry that weight a long time!"

"That's right, Johnny." I start tearing up, and he keeps on singing, "Carry that weight." It's one of those features of autism he has, getting stuck on a line.

"That's right, 'carry that weight,' Johnny. He sings louder and louder, rocking back and forth faster and more frantically. I pull the car over to the side of the road, halfway expecting him to have one of his blowups. "Please, Johnny!" I don't look at him. Instead, I put my arms around the steering wheel and lean forward with my head resting on my hands. I start bawling.

I feel his hand touching my shoulder, and I turn and look at him. He's looking at me straight in the eyes. His eyes have at once a look of pity and remoteness. I keep looking at his face, not trying to lock in on his eyes, but just enough to keep him engaged. "I love you, Johnny."

He turns and looks ahead through the windshield. "Go to store."

"Yeah." I turn on the blinker, signaling to get back on the road. "We're going to the store."

At around nine o'clock, I get on Skype with Seth. I haven't spoken to him in a while, since before Christmas. Usually we just pick up where we left off. I need a friend right now in a bad way.

"You know the girl I was going out with?" I wait to start this line of conversation after we talk about school for a little bit. "Emily?"

"Oh, yeah," he says casually, "how's that going?"

I almost cannot contain the quiver in my voice. I look up to keep the tears from falling out of my eyes. "We broke up."

"Oh," he says awkwardly. "That's too bad."

"She moved away." I wipe my nose. "But she doesn't want to stay in touch." I see him looking away from his Skype lens. "It just really hurts right now."

"Well, loss is painful," Seth finally says, summoning up the phrases his mother, the shrink, uses. But as trite as they may sound, anything sounds comforting to me now. "All loss means a certain amount of pain." He nods sympathetically.

"Yeah." I sniff a little bit and take a big breath. "It's hard."

"I know I'm not feeling good the next day after the Phillies lose." I look at Seth's image on my computer screen. I'm not sure whether he's being flippant or serious. Is he really equating my loss, my lost love, with the loss of a ball game? But then, that's all Seth's ever lost, really. And it's not even his game to lose. Somehow, that fact makes me feel better. Maybe the poet was right about never having loved at all.

We get back to talking about the upcoming baseball season and our fantasy picks. Thank God for sports.

Chapter 21

Elizabeth is in a funk. She may not be in as dark a mood as I was, but I can understand her being withdrawn. Having so-called friends post mean things about you tends to make you distrustful of everyone, and group therapy can do only so much. She loves to dance and won't give it up. That means the drama continues.

Mom volunteers at the SPCA once a week during school hours. She's never done foster care, as much as the dog fanatics and Elizabeth have tried to push it on her. "One dog is enough," she says. "Besides, I spend enough time away from Rosie to take care of other dogs, don't I, Rosie?" She walks over to the mutt lying on her dog bed and cups Rosie's head in her hands.

"Ah 'preciate all you do, Momma!"

Then Mom gets this notion that having her own special dog would be good therapy for my little sister, much in the way she thought a dog would help Johnny. Given all the trouble her dance team friends have caused her, having a dumb mutt to care for actually sounded like a good idea. As Dad once said, "in business, there is a saying: you want a friend, go get a dog." I can relate to that.

Mom approaches her as she sits on the sofa, reviewing her Pinterest page. "How would you like to get a little dog, sweetheart?"

Elizabeth bolts right up. "Yeah! That would be a great idea!" What is it about girls and puppies and horses? They go gaga about them. Mom tells her that they've got a dog at the shelter that's about to have a litter of puppies.

"But," Mom makes a caveat, "we need a docile dog, a little opposite of Rosie. A smaller dog, one that doesn't shed so much. I'll be on the lookout when one comes up." I'm standing at the island in the kitchen, making a sandwich as I take in this conversation. I shake my head. *We're not getting another dog! Not gonna happen.*

Elizabeth can see the ugliest things and think they are salvageable. She can look at one of Johnny's drawings and suggest to Mom that she frame it. She can look at the most uncoordinated kid at a dance camp for kids and tell her she has talent. In short, Elizabeth loves underdogs.

That's what she sees in this stray in our neighborhood. He is a black-and-white pit bull mix with droopy jowls and droopy ears that make him look sad. Or maybe he looks sad just because it was made clear to him that he is unwanted and has no place to go.

"Someone should call animal control," Mom says as we head to school one day and see the dog walking along the road like a hitchhiker.

"He's cute," Elizabeth says. "I feel sorry for him. No one wants him."

"He doesn't belong to anybody?" Mom asks. "I thought he belonged to that family on the corner. The father is a colonel in the marines or something."

"No," Elizabeth corrects her, "he's just a stray. I see him out when I'm on a run."

"Elizabeth, be careful! I hope he's never tried to bite you!"

"No, he usually runs away," she says. "I should take along some treats next time."

"No way!" Mom says. "The last thing we need is to have that dog following you home."

Lo and behold, this ugly mutt shows up at our door. I've seen him around the neighborhood, wandering around the streets while I'm driving. I figured he belonged to someone and they "accidentally" left their fence open. If he were my dog, I would have accidentally–on purpose left the gate open too.

As Mom pulls into the driveway of our house, there's that mutt parked right on our front porch. We can see Rosie in the dining room window, barking excitedly. She's got that happy look on her face, like she just made a new friend.

"Oh no!" she groans as she reaches up for the remote to open the garage. "I hate to call animal control, but there's nothing else we can do. You know they have dozens of these pit bulls and pit mixes that people just abandon. They don't get adopted."

"We can foster him," Elizabeth pleads.

"We don't do pit bulls," Mom says firmly.

"But he's so cute, Mom." Elizabeth is starting to sound like a lost puppy herself.

"He can't stay on our porch forever, sweetheart! I have to call animal control," Mom insists. "Maybe I can call People for Pits and see if they have any room for another one."

The lady at People for Pits tells her on the phone that there is no more space in any of their foster homes. That means it is up to Mother whether the mutt is going to live or die. The lady says she'll go to the pound the next day to check him out. Mom says she'll meet her there after her assessment.

"Well"—Mom's tone softens a bit as we head over to the county shelter—"if we do take him in, he's just going to live with us as a foster!"

"Look at him, Mom! Isn't he sweet?" Elizabeth gushes when we visit him in the animal shelter. *Sweet* isn't a word I would pin on a dog that looks like he has had his share of dogfights. He moves like a football tackle, hopping through tire rings at practice. He looks clumsy but tough.

The People for Pits lady gives us her assessment. "He's not a full-blooded pit, you know. I think he has some lab in him. Nice-looking dog, though. A real shame if we have to put him, you know, down."

160

"Mom, please!" Elizabeth pleads.

"Just as a foster!" Mom says firmly.

"He's kind of a smarty," I say on the way home. "Smarty Marty."

"That sounds like a good name. We'll call him Marty." Mom decides quickly. I think she doesn't want to spend too much time figuring out a name so Elizabeth won't get too attached to the ugly mutt. But the fact is, she already has.

Elizabeth and Mom go to the pet store and buy all kinds of dog toys and treats for the mutt, as if we are having a baby or something. They get him a brand-new collar and a tag with the name Marty engraved on it. It was my name that won out for some reason. I figured as dumb as he looks, he is still smart enough to find the one home in the neighborhood that wouldn't turn him away.

"What does Rosie say about this?" Elizabeth asks Mom.

"Rosie says, *'Give Marty a chance!'*"

At first Mom is rather reserved with the dumb mutt. "Marty, it's time to go out and relieve yourself," she says as she stands at the back door. She speaks to him as a teacher talking to a student she clearly doesn't like but tries hard not to show it.

"Thanks, Mom!" I hear a dopey-sounding voice as the dog walks by her. *"Uh, can I call you Mom?"*

"No, Marty!" Mom, in her split-personality way, talks back. "You are here for just a short time. Don't get too comfortable!"

"Wull, uh," the mutt answers, *"Uh just want to take this opportunity to thank you for saving my life and providing me with such a lovely home ... Mom."*

Chapter 22

Ms. Emerson is one of the nicer teachers when it comes to not making us have to take exams on exam week but just on a regular school day. She even let us take a "pretest," and if we had a good score, we could forgo taking the actual test.

"If you just use common sense, calculus is really easy," she always tells us, and someone in the class always says that's easy for her to say. Ms. Emerson is one of those math wizards. This stuff is child's play for her.

We start the pretest, and everyone has their head down and you can hear a pin drop—until the singing starts in the hallway. "I get by with a little help from my friends." Hand it to Johnny to break my concentration. And Ms. Emerson's. No one says anything, but I see her head bopping up and down to the song in her head.

"Do you need anybody? I just need someone to love," she sings quietly aloud.

"I just need someone to tell me the answers," sings this kid a few seats back in my row. Everyone starts laughing. Ms. Emerson looks up and laughs. "Hey," she says in a mocking serious tone, "you don't need that!" Then she sings, "You get by with a little stu-dy-ing!" Everyone starts laughing again, except one.

"How the hell am I supposed to concentrate with that kid making noise?" Blake snaps and then mutters, "Why do they have those kids here anyway?"

"All right, Blake!" Ms. Emerson says sternly.

Curtis, the kid next to him puts him in his place. "Blake, I don't think concentrating is your strong point anyway." I hear Blake whisper something that sounds like a curse. No one talks for the rest of the period.

After school we have one hour of wrestling practice—nothing much, just a short run around the school and working out on the weights. The days are longer now that it's spring, and maybe that's affecting my mood. I know grade-wise I did pretty well this year despite all the ups and downs in my life—mostly downs.

When practice lets out, I'm standing by the wall, waiting for Mom to come pick me up. And then Blake walks out, pushing the door open with such a force it looks as if it will come off. I don't think Blake did well on the pretest in math today. He always blames it on Johnny's singing, but it's just an excuse. The truth is the guy shouldn't be in that class in the first place. When it comes to academics, Blake is one of those guys who does just enough to appease his parents' wishes for him to get into an acceptable-enough college.

He looks around and sees me standing to the right of the double doors. Then without a word he walks past me, throws his gym bag and backpack down, and leans against the wall. He starts singing, clearly mocking Johnny. "Ah get by wit a widdle hep fwom my fwends." Over and over he sings it.

"Shut up, Blake," I say as neutrally as possible, not bothering to look at him.

So he starts singing it louder. "Ah get by wit a widdle hep fwom my fwends!"

"Yeah, that's real mature, Blake, making fun of a retarded kid." Maybe I shouldn't have used the "R" word, but I get the point across.

"Oh, wait a minute. Which one of you is the retard?" he asks, with the accent on the "re."

"Shut up, Blake!" I'm angry now.

"What are you gonna do, ugly?" he jeered. "I get by wit a widdle hep."

I lose it. I know that's not a valid excuse, but before I know it I grab him by surprise in a headlock and just start beating the crap out of him.

The surprise of it all prevents him from making an escape; normally it would be a move any novice wrestler should get out of. Realizing that I have him where I want him, I can't stop. He keeps trying to do a leg sweep on me, which is pointless because all it does is put him off balance.

"You mother—" He tries to talk but I keep at him. I am so intent on pinning him down on the concrete right there. He keeps pulling me over to the grassy area, as if that is out of bounds and he can stop the clock. But it just makes it easier for me to pick him up in a fireman's carry, throw him down on the ground, and pin him.

"Who are you calling retard, asshole?" I shout at him.

He can't answer. How long I hold him down for, I don't know. But behind me I hear Mom yelling, "No, Rosie! Marty, come back!"

Before I can think, there is Rosie to the rescue, though it is unclear at the time who she is trying to rescue.

"Get … off … me!" Blake's face is all screwed up as Rosie's big pink tongue is all over it.

He gets up just enough to be in the submission stance when Marty jumps on him and starts humping him.

"Get your damn dogs off me!" Blake screams.

Mom grabs hold of Marty's collar and then goes for Rosie's.

"Bad dogs!" she yells at them. "Are you okay?" she asks Blake in that freaked-out voice that Mom does so well. "I've got antibacterial wipes in the car."

She gets both dogs to go with her back to the car, and Blake gets up and looks at me with the usual hateful look; maybe this time the hate is a degree or two higher than normal, but since he always gave me those looks, I really can't tell.

By now I notice a crowd of about ten kids have gathered around. They are cheering. And laughing! Blake looks angry and humiliated.

"You're in big trouble, freak!" He looks straight at me.

"Oooh," someone says in mock horror. The crowd laughs. Mom returns with a plastic container of wipes and hands one to Blake, who knocks my mother's hand away with a look of disgust. She's taken aback at his rudeness but doesn't say anything about it. I think she realizes he's already in an angry state and doesn't want to stir things up.

"Well, I think I have to report this to Coach G," she says and heads for the gym. Blake and I give each other a quick look of alarm. I know he doesn't want this reported any more than I do.

"It's okay," he snaps. "It's no big deal."

"Yeah, Mom, it's no big deal," I say. "We were just grappling."

"That looked like more than just grappling!" She raises her voice. "I—"

"It's no big deal, I said!" Blake wipes his arms off, as if he's trying to wipe off the whole incident. I want to grab him and tell him, "Don't talk to my mother like that, you creep!" But I let it go. He's already headed off to get his backpack and gym bag by the wall.

Some kids are holding up their phones, recording all of this. *Great!* Blake's mother pulls up to the curb, and he heads to her car and gets in, and they're off.

"Don't you think his mother is going to want to talk to me?"

"No, Mom!" I say in as much a whisper as I can, knowing I'm being taped. "Let's go! Everybody's all right!" We get into the Highlander with the barking dogs. Johnny is sitting in the backseat, rocking back and forth. "Hi, Johnny, how was your day?" I ask, attempting to get back to normalcy. Mom and I go home in stunned silence. We're both thinking about the fallout that will come later. But it was clear when we left that Blake was okay physically—just a few of the usual scrapes anyone would get if they were on the mat. It was his ego that was bruised.

We pull into the garage, and Mom turns off the ignition. She smiles. "I'm proud of you," she tells me before she goes inside.

Dad calls and says he'll be home later than usual tonight due to some accident on the freeway. Mom alerts him to what happened after practice. He tells her we will talk about it first thing when he gets home.

The rest of us have already eaten when Dad finally gets home. "Have a seat, Benjamin," he says after he puts his briefcase away. He and Mom take a seat next to each other on the sofa. I sit in the big chair in the corner, waiting to be questioned about the day's events. Johnny is sitting on the sofa in the sunroom. I can see him out of the corner of my eye. He looks tense, but at least he's quiet. Elizabeth is sitting at the kitchen table, supposedly doing her homework.

Mom gives Dad a sympathetic account of the fight with Blake. "I'm proud of the way Benjamin stuck up for his brother," she says.

"I just hope nothing comes of this, like a suspension," Dad says. "That wouldn't look good on your record. I don't know how a prospective college would look at this."

"Don't worry about it, Dad," I say, trying to sound like it's no big deal.

"That's easy for you to say, Benjamin!" He raises his voice at me. "What if his parents decide to charge you with assault? Or if they accuse us of letting our pit bull attack him?"

"He wasn't hurt!" Mom insists. "I saw it. In fact, there were lots of people who saw it. Some of those kids were recording it with their phones!"

"Oh, great!" Dad throws his head back. "We're going to be in big trouble!"

"This will give evidence that Marty and Rosie didn't hurt him, Keith!" Mom says. Nice that she's thinking of the dogs! *Hey, Mom, I might need a little help with my defense too!*

Elizabeth butts in, "They better not do anything to Marty! He didn't do anything. He just hopped on Blake and hopped off."

"How do you know, Elizabeth?" Mom asks. "You weren't there!"

"Millie posted it on her Facebook page." We all get up and head over to get a look on Elizabeth's laptop. There it is, complete with comments from guys on the team and other people who don't know.

"Look!" Mom says. "Read those comments. 'Those are cute dogs!'"

Dad laughs as he reads another. "Blake likes it doggy style!"

"Ooo, he's not gonna like that!" I shake my head. So far, there are about ninety likes and several shares. It is a posting that definitely will receive the attention of the school administration. We try to find some other postings or links to find out who originally posted it. Turns out it is some guy from the track team. The video doesn't show who started the fight, so I am thinking maybe I will be lucky and Blake can't prove that I started it. But then, I remember there were other people there who witnessed the whole thing.

"Just tell Dr. Hemphill the truth, Benjamin," Dad says. "Tell him how Blake punched you in practice. Tell him how he's been bullying you these past two years."

"That wouldn't matter now, anyway, Dad."

"Yes, it would!" Mom interjects. "And you have witnesses that saw him punch you in practice."

"You just tell the truth, Benjamin," Dad says. "The truth will win out."

From out of the sunroom, Johnny jumps up, shaking. He has that mad look on his face—meaning he's going to explode.

"Johnny?" Mom tries to sound calm and walks over to him. "Johnny, use your words. What is wrong, Johnny? What do you want?" He growls like an animal. "Johnny," she repeats, "use your words—"

He grabs Mom and starts kicking her. "Johnny! No!" She tries to hold him back. She's helpless by herself. I bolt over there with Dad right with me. Johnny comes after me. He's looks like a crazed monster.

These episodes come out of the blue. The last time he had one was last semester when school first started. He was in his classroom, so at least he didn't make a scene in the hallway. He ended up giving his teacher a bruise on her arm, and the teacher's assistant sprained his arm. And this is a big guy. When Johnny's like this he has the strength of a wild beast.

"Grab him! Hold his arms down!" Mom screams.

"Take him down!" Dad shouts. Johnny's writhing and shaking on the floor. Dad and I are holding him down in a pin, only we have to keep him in a pin for at least five minutes before he calms down. After a few minutes, I try letting up but he tries to attack so I put him back into a pin.

"Keep holding him," Dad says, almost out of breath. "I got his legs." Don't ask what brings these things on. It's just part of the wonderful world of autism. "We've got to do something. Put him on medication," Dad says. Mom is shaking and crying.

"I know," she says with a tone of surrender.

What a day. I put both Blake and Johnny in a pin. I wish it counted for something.

I can't sleep. The whole scene with Blake keeps replaying in my head. I wonder if anybody at school will speak up for me. As faces of J. T. and Mike pop into my head, I see them just turning away, as if they want to have nothing to do with me. But then, maybe not. Maybe I will finally get some respect around the team. I mean, things can't get any worse as far as my standing around there goes.

On the other hand, who knows if I will still even be on the team? I know what I did would be considered assault by the school. In my father's time, it would have been considered just two guys working out their differences. Too bad I didn't live in that era. What's so crazy is that the coaches want us to be aggressive on the mat and the teachers want us to be as gentle and quiet as lambs. I'm not going to be a sheep anymore, I decide, not when there are wolves like Blake. Actually, calling Blake a wolf is an insult to wolves. He's a much lower animal than that.

Chapter 23

There are about a dozen kids already in Ms. Emerson's class when I come in. All eyes are on me except Ms. Emerson's; she's putting up some problems on the board. I manage to catch Talia, the girl who sits behind me, looking at me, with a hint of a smile. I smile back at her briefly.

Someone coughs, but other than that you can hear a pin drop.

"Nice picture of you and your dog, Ben," Talia says as she taps me on the back of my shoulder.

I turn around to see her scrolling for the picture on her phone. She lets me sneak a peek before she puts her phone away in her purse. There I am on the right-hand side of the picture, holding Rosie in my arms. On the left side is the backside of Marty with his front legs raised up on Blake. Not to sound like a braggart, but that wild, roughed-up look serves me well. Talia gives me a satisfactory smile. "What's your dog's name?"

"Rosie," I whisper. "Uh, thanks … for showing me."

"She's a pretty dog," Talia whispers back and then adds, "You don't look too bad either!" *Wow.* Maybe there's an upside to this!

Blake comes in looking straight ahead. There are a few snickers and clearing of throats. The phone on Ms. Emerson's desk rings, and she picks it up. "Yes, they are both in here." She looks at me quizzically and glances at Blake. "Okay, yes, sir.

"Ben, Mr. Strong wants to see you in his office." I get up, but my legs are wobbly. Between fighting Blake and having to restrain Johnny yesterday, my body is feeling the aftershocks. I turn around to get Blake's reaction: a smug smile. I catch Talia giving me a warm smile, as if to say, "Good for you." I wait until I get in the hall to let out a big sigh.

I go into Mr. Strong's office, and he invites me to have a seat. He seems really nice, or at least he sounds that way over the intercom when he's giving the morning announcements. I really only know him from seeing him walking in the halls, smiling at everyone, occasionally giving out a high five. He is on the small side and slightly built. Unlike J. T., I can't get away with trying to sound like "a brotha" and look cool around Mr. Strong, so I don't try.

"Why don't you tell us your side of the story, Benjamin?" Mr. Strong asks, although there is no "us," only him. "Or is it Ben?"

"I go by both," I tell him.

"Which one would you prefer I call you?"

"Either one."

"Okay, Benjamin," he said with a sigh, "suppose you tell me what's going on with you and Blake Barker. There's a video of it that has apparently gone viral on Facebook, Instagram, Twitter, and all those other places kids post things on. So keep that in mind." He breaks out in a big grin.

"I know that, sir. What the video doesn't show is Blake making fun of my brother, Johnny. Johnny has autism, and he likes to sing."

"Oh, *that* Johnny. He's your brother?"

"Yes, sir." I make a mental note that I might be able to win some sympathy by being the brother of Johnny—make that the defender of Johnny and all the disabled kids out there. "Well, if you've ever heard my brother around here, he likes to sing."

"So you're Johnny's brother?" he asked, and I nodded. Mr. Strong puts on a look of pity. "That must be kind of hard living with a brother with special needs."

"I guess so," I say, trying to imitate Mom's martyr look.

"I enjoy his music." He smiles, as if that will lighten the atmosphere a bit. "He sings that song 'We don't need no education!' You know which song I'm talking about?"

"Yes, sir." I smile as his head bops to the rhythm of the Pink Floyd song in his head.

"I wonder sometimes if he's trying to tell us something." Mr. Strong looks at me, as if there is some big mystery going on in Johnny's head. "You know? Like, we don't *need* education. We don't *need* thought control. Hmm."

"Yes, sir." I nod. "Johnny's a mystery."

"Well, son"—Mr. Strong puts on this pained look that I can't tell for sure is real—"I hate to have to do this. But you and Blake Barker made some bad choices. Dr. Hemphill is going to want to talk to both of you and your parents, as well."

"But if you knew what Blake has—"

"I know, I know." Mr. Strong puts his hand up to silence me. "But we can't have fighting going on at North Central, no matter whose fault it is. That's how it is, Benjamin." I'm about to say something, but I can see he wants to get rid of me. He stands up and tells me to go back and sit in the waiting area for Dr. Hemphill.

I meet Blake outside of the principal's office, where the secretary sits. She goes into his office and comes out after a few minutes. She closes the door and looks at us officiously. "You may go back to your classes, until we can contact your parents. You will both stay out of trouble, won't you?" She adjusts her eyeglasses, giving us a condescending look.

Right before school is about to let out, I am summoned to the principal's office once again. This time both Mom and Dad are there. I'm told Blake and his parents are being held in a separate holding area, probably in the main office. Mom greets me with a hug.

"How's it going, son?" Dad pats me on the back, trying to appear as unperturbed as possible.

"I'm okay," I say insouciantly, one of the words for the week in my English class. The word has a nice ring to it, an I-couldn't-care-less-about-this ring.

Blake and I are called in first. Dr. Hemphill is sitting behind his desk, and there are two small armchairs in front of the desk. He waves his arm, motioning us to sit in the chairs. He inspects us for a moment. "I don't want to know who started it," Dr. Hemphill starts off without the formalities. "I'm finishing it."

That really ticks me off. Everybody's entitled to a hearing. My future is now being decided by this tall thin-haired bureaucrat wearing a collared dress shirt and tie. He has a smug look of superiority that a lot of those administrative types have.

"What do you mean?" I raise my voice. "You don't care who started it?"

"It doesn't matter, son," he cuts me off.

I kick his desk almost involuntarily, as if I get kicked right below the knee. "It does matter who started it!" I look right at him, my jaw so tight I almost can't feel it.

"Young man, you will calm down right now," the man says in a low threatening tone. I've never been in trouble. I've always kept my head down and kept doing what I was supposed to do. Has that earned me any respect? Not by this guy. I am just a number to him, a cog in the wheel. So I decide to challenge him a little.

"Are you saying if someone taunted your daughter, made fun of your disabled son, punched your kid day in and day out, month after month, and you decide one day that you would man up and fight back for once, that none of those circumstances matter?" I wait for an answer. He just ignores me.

"Well, if that's the case," I conclude my argument, "if it doesn't matter to you, then it doesn't matter to me what you have to say." I get up and start to leave.

"Sit down." He gives me a stern look at first, but then I can see him softening a bit. "I'll go over the procedures of handling altercations with you." His focus is all on me up until now. Then he looks at Blake, as if he has forgotten about the dummy sitting in the chair beside me, who has been uncharacteristically silent in defending himself. "I'll explain it to you both." He gives a nod to Blake, who smirks back. It seems to be the only way he knows how to express any kind of satisfaction.

I refuse to give in and be conciliatory. "Why should I listen to you?" I challenge, asking in the most respectful tone I can muster.

"Because I am the principal, young man!" The corner of my lip starts to turn up into a smile as I see him trying to control his temper.

"I guess that makes a difference to you." I nod at him, as if I am speaking to a little kid. I'm starting to turn the tables on him. And Blake's just sitting there, not knowing what to make of any of this.

"Yes, it makes a big difference!" He smirks back at me.

"Well"—I start to crescendo—"it makes a big difference who started it!"

I look over at Blake, who's got this scared look on his face. I decide to cash in all my chips and go for it. I've got nothing to lose anyway. I turn my attention to Blake. "You don't have anything to worry about, Blake. North Central loves bullies like you, don't you, Dr. Hemphill? Just ask that kid who killed himself on YouTube last year. He was going on about being bullied at North Central. That was really good publicity for the school, wasn't it? They harbor bullies at North Central!"

I know I've cornered the principal when he makes a feeble defense. "Well, we can't know what's going on everywhere."

"That's why I want you to listen to my case." Now I'm feeling like a lawyer! "I don't deserve to get suspended. Blake and I will show you—do a little reenactment here—how he sucker punches me and other kids at practice. You can play Coach G, conveniently looking the other way. Then, we'll—"

"Okay, Benjamin," he says, "I've heard what I need to hear. I'm going to talk to your parents. We'll get this resolved. Please understand that there are procedures that I have to follow. By law. But I have to say I'm really disappointed that two kids on the same team can't get along."

"He started it!" I won't back down. "He's the bully! He's the instigator in all of this!"

"Shut up!" Blake snaps.

"That's enough!" Hemphill shouts. He inhales a gallon of air and lets it out slowly. We all sit in silence for a minute. I look at Blake, who is looking down at the carpet. Then I see Hemphill staring at his desk. I look around. I think I've made an impression around here. Dr. Hemphill reaches for the telephone and tells the secretary to have Mr. and Mrs. Barker come in his office in five minutes. I'm dismissed to sit out with Mom and Dad. They both give me cautious but encouraging smiles.

Dad, Mom, and I are sitting in the waiting area for what seems like half an hour when Blake and his parents exit the principal's office. Blake's father turns back and points his finger at Dr. Hemphill. "This better get off my son's record." The principal gives a look like he's heard it before.

Blake's father then gives my father a contemptuous look, turns around, and heads out, with his wife looking slightly embarrassed, whispers, "Come on, Blake."

After they leave, Dad, Mom, and I go back into the office and the principal delivers his verdict to us.

"I am bound by law to suspend both the boys," he says, sounding a lot more congenial and sympathetic with my parents. "But rather than having them spend that time at home, I have an assignment for them. A bonding exercise." I try to suppress a smirk forming on my mouth.

"For two hours, they will spend time together in a public place—a restaurant, library, whatever we decide—and they will sit at a table and talk. Without any cell phones or any electronic devices. Two hours. And I want a written report of what went on. Five hundred words. If I get that, the suspensions will be expunged from their records."

My parents just sit there quietly. But I see the gears turning inside my dad's head. Mom is looking at him as though she's thinking, *Please don't cause a scene.*

"Well, you know it's the other kid's fault, right?" Dad asks. "I mean, off the record, you know that should matter." The principal smiles and says nothing. Dad gets up, shakes his hand, and thanks him for being lenient with me. *What the ...* I'm thinking.

On the way back home in Dad's car, the three of us look out the windows in silence. As Dad turns onto the main road leading to our subdivision, he says, "You know, Benjamin, that coach at All Saint's School really liked your wrestling."

"When was this?" Mom asks. As usual, she's not in tune with my wrestling.

"It was at the tournament two weeks ago," Dad says. "He told me he wished he could have you on his team. He said he could get some scholarship money for you."

"That's nice," I say without much enthusiasm. The thought of going to a boarding school doesn't appeal to me. If I can't fit in at North Central, how could I fit in at a boarding school?

"He's a really good guy. And that's a good school. They turn out some good wrestlers."

"Yeah, I beat their kid." I smile as I recall that match. He seemed like a nice guy. I can always get a sense of the guys who are good competitors, meaning they take it seriously without getting eaten up about winning. Maybe Dad is right.

"I don't know if that would be the right thing to do for his senior year," Mom says, throwing a wet blanket on the idea.

"We'll talk more about it later," Dad says. "I just think if Benjamin can go somewhere where he can get lots of matches and compete on the A team ..."

"You mean, he'll be a big fish in a small pond," Mom clarifies, taking the spin out of Dad's proposal.

"Well, yeah," Dad says, "kind of. But this crap about him having to do this suspension is just the stuff I get tired of. It was the other kid's fault. He's been like this the whole time Benjamin has been at North Central. And yet, they both get into trouble. It's a bunch of bull."

"Yeah, that's true," Mom says. "But what can we do? I'd rather fight the system than run away."

"That's what I tried to do Mom, and look where it got me," I pipe up. It just makes me realize how much I can't wait to get out of school, to get out of this stupid town.

Dad pulls the car into the garage and turns off the ignition. "Don't worry about this thing with Blake, okay, Benjamin? We'll take care of it."

"That's okay, Dad. I'll be all right," I say with slight irritation. I don't need him solving my problems. On the other hand, the other source of my irritation is the way I'm being treated by Dr. Hemphill and the school. I just wish he would hear me out. Benjamin McDowell does not equal Blake Barker. Trying to get that through his crap-filled PhD brain is a waste of time.

We get home, and I go sit in the sunroom with Marty, Rosie, and Johnny. I don't know if I want to give Marty a big hug or kick him. He's lying on his bed on the floor with his head between his paws. He looks up at me with these big bug eyes. It's hard to stay angry with a dog.

"Thorry about duh Blake-mounting incident!" I hear Mom behind me, interpreting the mutt's thoughts. In the past few months, Marty has had lots of "incidences" to apologize for: *"Thorry about the burrito-eating incident, Mom! Thorry about eating the brownies. They looked like little burgers!" "Thorry about the*

counter-surfing incident! But thumpting sure smelled good up there."
"Thorry about the cat-chasing incident! I thought he wanted to play!"
Mom always manages to forgive him.

"Well, that's okay, Marty." I smile and pet him. "Everything will work out for the best. At least, that's what I'm told."

"Well, *uh, it seemed like a good idea at the time! Then I figured, he wasn't worth it!"* Marty lying on his dog bed, his expression mirroring Mom's words. Mom puts her hand on my shoulder. We sit on the floor, petting the dogs.

"Do you think Marty would have—could have—really hurt Blake?" I ask. "I mean, you know what they say about pit bulls."

"Marty is only part pit," Mom says in his defense. "Plus, I contacted Trudy, the lady who runs Pits for People. She said it's all in the way a dog has been brought up."

"I heard sometimes they just turn on you," I counter, "they" being pit bulls, but then I think about people who've turned on me, namely Emily. "I guess people can do that too, can't they? Just turn on you."

I hear Dad coming out of the office. "I e-mailed the coach," Dad says, sounding upbeat. "We'll see what happens."

In the meantime, I have to work on putting this "talk out" with Blake behind me.

We both agree to meet at Adele's Corner. It is busy enough most of the time, so I figure Blake won't make a scene. Plus, there is a television there, usually playing the sports channel.

"Call or text me if there are any problems," Dad says before he leaves for work. "I'm proud of you, son."

Mom nods. "Don't let him get to you. Remember, he's not worth it." I smile a little and tell her not to worry. She gives me a hug.

I get there first. It's a little before ten in the morning. I look around to make sure I haven't overlooked him. I stand in the short line to order just a drink. I'm still looking for Blake, but I still don't see him. We agreed on ten, but he has a few minutes. I get my Coke and go sit at a table for two by the window, next to the front door. I sit facing the door so I can see him.

Blake arrives a few minutes after ten. I recognize the red Ford Fiesta pulling into the parking spot facing away from the restaurant. It has a "North Central Wrestling" sticker on the rear windshield. He gets out sporting a surly look.

"Hey, Blake!" I call out to him. "I'm over here." He's a little pissed that I have a table already, as if I've already marked my territory and he has to come sit in it. He smirks and starts heading toward me.

"All right, let's get this over with," he mumbles. I wonder if he's trying to make a statement with his disheveled appearance, but I decide I don't care. I pull out my notebook and start writing.

"Blake enters, looking like he just got out of bed ..." I say as I write.

"What the f—"

"We've got to write a report, remember?" I smile sarcastically. "And let's not forget we are here to talk things out like the rational human beings we are."

"Wow, you're really taking this very seriously, aren't you?" He rolls his eyes as he shakes his head. "Look, I'm sorry if I hurt your brother and you. I have an uncle who's like your brother. I know how it is."

It's my turn to roll my eyes: "I wish I had a dime for every time someone told me they knew someone with autism or 'someone like your brother.'"

"I was just trying to be sympathetic." He folds his arms and looks away. He looks sincere, so I try to backtrack to press him a little.

"Do you see your uncle much?"

"No, I hardly ever see him." Blake stares at my drink, speaking in a flat tone. "He's in a home. My aunt sees him. He doesn't have autism. He got brain damage from a car accident. My father was driving the car. It was a long time ago. I don't really remember

179

it." He looks down at the floor and changes the subject. "Did you bring a chessboard?"

"Yeah, I figured we could play to pass the time. I could teach you how." He gives me his signature smirk. I'm trying my best to be friendly, to reach out. Okay, so maybe bringing chess wasn't the best idea. But I figured he wasn't much into board games anyway.

"You know Best Buy is right over there." He gives me a mock-serious look. "I heard they're looking for more geeks for their squad."

"Real clever," I sneer at him. Blake's hopeless. This is going to be a long two hours. "So why don't you ever see your uncle?"

"He lives in Maryland." Blake is starting to look uncomfortable. I like that.

"That's not that far! I have uncles who live all over the place, and I see them every year."

"He doesn't know me! He doesn't know anything." Blake shrugs. "And I don't know him. So what's the point?"

"Do you remember him?" I'm really curious now. Maybe this will give me some insights into his character. "Before the accident?"

"I told you it was a long time ago!" Blake snaps. "What is this? You're writing a book?" He turns in his seat and looks out the window for a few seconds. "I'm getting something to eat." He gets up and heads toward the counter.

"Hurry back!" I smile at him sarcastically. He mouths an "F-you!" back at me, which gets me laughing. I might like this after all! "We still have another hour and forty-five minutes!"

Blake comes back with a chocolate chip cookie and an iced coffee. He's looking real cocky. "So I heard you are thinking of not coming back to North Central next year. Can't handle the competition, huh?"

Man, how rumors spread. I texted J. T., Mike, and a few other guys on the team about my dad looking into sending me there, and that's all it takes. "Actually, Blake, I was approached by the coach at All Saints. He's very impressed by my abilities. A little jealous?"

Score a point for that escape!

"Oooh, rich boy going to private school!" he sneered. He turns in his seat, out toward the counter, and takes a big bite of his cookie.

"I was being recruited, Blake. I haven't made up my mind yet." I certainly am not going to tell him my plans.

"Look, why don't we play a game of chess just to pass the time? I don't want to be here any more than you do, but we may as well—"

"Shut up!" he snaps without bothering to look at me. *Don't tell me to shut up, Blake!* But I hold my tongue for a minute, trying to figure out how to get the time to go by quicker. Then I realize why not get to the crux of the whole matter?

"Why do you hate me so much?" I ask matter-of-factly. He doesn't answer. He doesn't even move. It's as if he wants to look like he won't deign to give me his attention.

"I know why I don't like you." I take charge of things. "You're a cheater, a bad sport, full of contempt for people."

"I'm just full of contempt for you," he sneers.

"Why? I haven't done anything to you." I'm still calm—at least I think so on the outside.

"It's just who you are and what you are!" Blake jerks around in his chair slightly. "You're a nerd. You read all the time. You think you're better than everyone else! Well, you're not. I bet you're a virgin!"

I'm bound and determined not to let that remark get to me. "Well, I can tell you right now, Blake, I'm not interested in you."

"Oh, that's funny," he smirks.

"Besides, I can't afford to catch crabs, or whatever it is they say you've got."

"See what I mean? You're a real asshole," he says, looking slightly hurt, as if I am the only one slinging insults.

"You started it!" I jab every word at him. I decide to go back and write some more notes for the report I have to hand in to Dr. Hemphill, which gets Blake irritated.

"We may as well play some chess." He sighs as if he is really putting himself out. "Just keep in mind I don't spend hours playing with chess idiots on the Internet."

"I like to call them 'chessnuts,' Blake." I smile sarcastically. He smirks. I set up the board. I let him be white. At least Blake has a cursory knowledge of how the game is set up and what each piece can do. But he is definitely a novice, and he isn't playing in a competitive mood. He moves his pawns in a haphazard way, clearly not giving it much thought. He moves his rook to the left.

"Check," he says.

"You know I can get you," I tell him, but then maybe he doesn't.

"Oh, right." He looks for a safe move. I move my right pawn up a little. The concentration is killing him so he flips his hand and knocks over a piece.

"You know you play chess the way you wrestle, Blake. If it doesn't work out your way, just knock over the pieces. Just do a sucker punch. Bitch slap your opponent."

"That's BS."

"It's true, and you know it." I put away the chess pieces and fold up the board. "It might be better to think things through."

"I beat you in the play-offs." He tries to trump me.

"You cheated and then you got disqualified at the Woodbridge tournament for doing the same thing!"

"At least I got there!" he snaps.

I shake my head. There is nothing more to say. I don't care anymore if Blake likes me. Blake is a bully. There is no common ground with us. I can't appeal to any sense of fairness or honesty. Empathy or compassion is not in his repertoire. Only fear and intimidation. So I end our painfully awkward meeting speaking his language.

"If I ever hear you, or hear of you, making fun of my brother, I am taking the gloves off and I'm going to punch you so hard you'll be joining your uncle in that home." I look him right in the eyes. He just sneers back.

"One of us will be dead before that happens."

"Oh, you want to die, huh?" I ask without missing a beat. I pause briefly. "No, Blake. I don't want to kill you. I just want you to hurt for a long time."

The alarm on my phone goes off, just in time.

"Well, time's up," I say as I swipe my phone to turn it off. I get up and leave.

I'm driving back home and see Mom walking Marty and Rosie along the street that leads to our street. I wave to her from the car. She waves back. I stop and roll down the window. She walks up, gathering the leashes in one hand.

"Hi." I give a half smile and rest my elbow on the door. "Want a ride?"

"Sure," she says. I pop open the hatch, and Marty jumps right in. Rosie's back legs are getting stiff, so we usually open the side door so she can take small steps. "Rosie is acting funny. She keeps rubbing her head against my leg."

"It's probably just her allergies," I assure Mom as we climb in the car.

"How did it go?" she asks as she puts on her seat belt.

"Okay." I put the car in drive and head home.

"What does that mean? Okay?" she asks with a little impatience.

"Just okay, Mom. I'll tell you about it when we get home."

"Just tell me now." I'm hoping to just brush her inquiries aside, but she won't let up. "I'm not asking you, 'How was school today?' I'm asking you—"

"Nothing happened, Mom!" I insist. "We just talked a little."

"Did he apologize?" she demanded. "Is he able to see what he did? Did you come to some kind of understanding—"

"Yes," I cut her off. "We came to an understanding. Are we friends? No. But it's okay. We agreed to disagree. We agreed to be civil. And that was it." Of course I downplayed the whole thing. I didn't want to get the third degree from my mother. She wouldn't understand anyway.

Somewhat satisfied, she lets me leave it at that. "Well, you're going to have to write that up in five hundred words!"

"I know, Mom." I pull into the garage and help her get Rosie out.

"Poor thing." Mom sounds worried and gives Rosie a big hug. "These allergies are really getting to her."

"Ah jes need to rest, Momma."

I can't decide whether I should write a snarky essay telling Dr. Hemphill how stupid I think this whole exercise is or just write a bunch of BS about how talking things out makes everything better and how Blake and I are best friends now. I decide on merging the two: make it so over the top that even Hemphill, with all his degrees, can't miss my satire.

Maybe going to this private school is just what I need. I have always felt like I don't belong at North Central. The guys on the wrestling team never understood me, and I like to think I'm mature enough to be able to look at my situation in an objective manner. I'm just a geek who happens to be pretty good at sports. I know there must be some other guys like me, but they keep their geekiness hidden. To be honest, I feel like I'm copping out a little too, like I'm some rich boy who needs to be protected from the rough world. Plus, I feel guilty about the expense of it. I get that from my mother, I know. It's bad enough I don't have a job, and now I'd be spending their extra money. Oh, well, it's Dad's idea anyway. That's why I can't wait to get out of here. I want to make my own decisions.

It's the week before exam week, when most of the nice teachers give out the exam so you won't have to show up for just half a day. Ms. Emerson is giving her final exam. The real one. Hardly anyone did well on that prefinal, except Curtis who scraped by with a B. He's the kid who sits next to Blake and makes wisecracks when Blake complains about Johnny.

"Now just remember everything we went over," Ms. Emerson says. "And relax. You should be able to do this test in ten minutes, but I'm giving you the entire period."

"Maybe ten minutes is enough for you, Ms. Emerson," says Curtis. "It might take me twenty."

"I could figure this out in two minutes." She waves her hand dismissively. "Really. I'm almost embarrassed to give you all such an easy test." She and Curtis act like this is so simple, so elementary. I envy Curtis. I wish I could get to know him better. I wonder if he plays chess. But I don't have his ability to figure things out so easily, so I get back to the exam.

Then, just like you know thunder is going to sound before it does, here comes Johnny. "Good-bye, yellow brick roh-oh-ohd!"

"Aaahh, ah-ah-ah-ah!" Ms. Emerson sings in a whisper. My shoulders hunch up a little, waiting for Blake to say something, but he doesn't. At least that's one little victory.

Chapter 24

It's Saturday, and graduation is next week. Already Mom and Elizabeth have planned this big party for Johnny and his classmates (all four of them). It's not like Johnny is really going anywhere, except to the other high school that has the "postgraduate" program. In other words, they try to teach Johnny and his friends how to do menial work so that he can get a job at Goodwill or something.

Oh, well. After all that's happened to me this year, I will be glad to graduate in my own way from North Central. It will be interesting to see so many people at the football stadium next Saturday for the ceremony. Maybe I'll get a chance to tell some people good-bye.

Mom and Elizabeth are making a big deal about it. "Mom, I saw this neat idea on Pinterest," Elizabeth says as she is coming down the stairs into the kitchen with a plastic box of old pictures. "We get all of his school pictures from K to 12, make copies, and hang them up for decorations.

"Oh, that sounds nice," Mom says in a flat tone. I'm sitting at the island in the kitchen while she's looking for other ideas. A look of sadness comes over her face for a moment before she suddenly sees something.

"Elizabeth, look at this!" Now she's smiling. "You take Reese's Peanut Butter Cups and top them off with a square of Hershey's chocolate bar by sticking a toothpick with a tassel through them. It looks like a graduation cap."

"Yeah, I saw those. They're all over Pinterest," Elizabeth says, like the idea is so yesterday. She puts down the box of pictures and stands beside Mom to look at more ideas.

"Well, we also need to start cleaning up," Mom says to everyone.

"Mom, it's a week away." I shake my head slightly.

"This house is so messy. It's going to take that long," Mom nags. I hate it when we have people over. She freaks out every time about how messy the house is. She spends days vacuuming and dusting just to have it all come back. But mostly, I hate the way she gets on me: "Clean the toilets on the first floor and in the basement, Benjamin! And be sure to go under the rim! Use gloves!"

Mom puts us to work as soon as we get home from school Friday, the day of the party.

"You missed getting all of the stairs," she says to me after I vacuumed most of the downstairs. I mean, it's not like people are going to inspect the whole house. And most of them are like Johnny, so what difference does it make?

"Go back and vacuum some more. And get all your papers that are scattered all over the place. I don't know which ones are good and which to throw away. Now!"

"I can't wait to get out of this house!" I say loud enough to hear over sounds of frantic activity.

"I can't wait for you to leave either." She starts up the basement stairs, shaking like she is about to cry. She starts running like she's desperately trying to get away from something. I start wondering if all this turmoil set Johnny off. I go upstairs to get ready to pull him off of her.

I hear the door off the sunroom slam, and I look out the family room window from a distance. She's on the deck. She's sitting on a patio chair, hugging Rosie. Her whole body is shaking. Elizabeth, in the middle of dusting off the furniture in the family room, looks out of the window.

"Go out there and make sure she's okay." Elizabeth looks at me accusingly.

"Why don't you?" I retort. "She doesn't care what I have to say."

"So what?" She raises her voice slightly. "Why can't you just help out instead of giving her a hard time? You have to talk to her. You are the one who is upsetting her!"

"There's nothing I can say!" I shake my head and throw my hands up.

"Just go!" Elizabeth says through gritted teeth. "Tell her you are sorry!"

Mom looks so pathetic out there, hugging that old mutt while the other one lies in the shaded area of the deck. I may as well get this over with.

"Hi," I say after I step out and shut the door. She's sniffling and heaving. She wipes her snot with the cleaning rag she's been carrying around.

"Sorry I upset you," I say to break the silence. "I know I'm a messy kid." She just stares at Rosie's ears. "That's the good thing about going to this school. It'll teach me—"

"Why am I celebrating?" she asks through deep breaths. "After years of going to speech therapy, play therapy, this therapy, and that therapy, after spending so much time fighting with the schools to get him more services, what did we get in the end? Johnny doesn't talk any better than he did when he was little." She begins sobbing again, clutching Rosie even tighter. Rosie just sits there, letting Mom slobber all over her.

"That's okay, Mom" is all I can say. I shift from one foot to the other, hoping she'll calm down soon.

"So maybe he can tell you his phone number if you ask him," she continues, "or he can name colors and types of transportation." Johnny is really crazy about trains and helicopters. He really gets excited when he sees a helicopter or when we come to the train tracks. "Is that a reason to celebrate?"

I don't know what to say. I mean, what can I say? Everything she said is true. There's really nothing to celebrate. Johnny is never going to change for the better. It's like that fact has finally dawned on Mom. But I put on a happy attitude and give her a quick pat on the shoulder. "We'll just have a good time just to have a good time, Mom."

"I want to be able to talk to my son!" She takes in a deep breath and looks over toward the sunroom, seeing her adult son rocking back and forth with his iPod. "I don't want a son like that!" She puts her fingers over her mouth. "That's awful!" She starts crying again. "I don't mean that."

"Of course you do, Mom," I say. I think about Blake and what he said about his uncle. He was right in a sense. Maybe it's better to be dead than to be a person who serves no purpose. "Who would want a kid like Johnny? That's just being honest."

"Don't say that!" Mom wails. "Of course I wouldn't give Johnny up for anything! But if I could just have him be a kid who talked, even if he talked back to me or was sarcastic with me—just a normal kid—I would cut off my right arm for that!"

"Well, you do have a son like that!" I snap at her. "Me!" I look at her, ticked off. "And do you care about me? No! All you ever cared about were Johnny and that dog!"

"That's not true, Benjamin!" she shoots back at me. We're back to our regular mode of conversation. "You get treated like a prince around here! You get—"

"By Dad! He only cares about my wrestling. You don't even care about that! All you say is that you want me to get out of here!"

"I say that because … isn't that what you want?" She looks vehemently at me. "I do all I can to make sure you are independent, teach you how to drive, mow the lawn, learn how to fix a dinner so that you can go out on your own—"

"Because you want me out of here!"

"Because that's the way it's supposed to be!" She starts crying again, which throws me off, and I can't think of anything to say. That gives her time to collect her thoughts. *Is this the way all women manipulate men?*

"You're supposed to grow up and be a man," she says quietly. "Be on your own. Don't you know what a precious gift that is? To make your own decisions? Make your own money? Think for yourself?"

I sit down in the chair next to hers. We both run out of steam. I give Rosie a pat on the shoulder. Rosie doesn't take any of this fighting to heart. She just lies next to Mom with her front paws out and her head up. She's panting, making her smiley face.

"Ah love my human puppies!"

"Dogs don't talk, Mom."

"Rosie does," she insists as she hugs the old dog's neck. "Don't you, girl? And she cares about you. Wants to protect you. Wants to love you."

"Well, I love Rosie too," I say with a reluctant smile. I put my arm around Mom as a way of saying I want a truce. She puts hers around me and gives me a squeeze. I give her shoulders a squeeze.

"Ow!" She pushes back a little. "Benjamin, I'm not a wrestler!"

"Sorry, Mom." I release her a little but still hold on, and she caresses my arm. We hold each other in silence for a few seconds.

"Oh my God," she moans suddenly, remembering the party. "Everyone's coming around six. I'm not ready! The place is still not straightened up!"

"Don't worry about it, Mom." I let out a short laugh. "They're autistic kids. They don't care about how clean the house is!"

"I think some of them have obsessive-compulsive issues," she frets, looking at me helplessly, "like cleanliness!"

"Then let them clean the house!" I put my arm back around her.

"And what about their parents? And the teachers? They're going to think I'm an awful housekeeper."

"They are probably glad you're having a party for their kids!" I assure her. "Now come on. Let's go back inside." I stand up and extend my hand. She takes it and pulls herself up.

"Thank you, son." She pats me on the shoulder and wipes her face one last time as we head back inside.

The party is actually kind of fun. Elizabeth and Mom came up with this "Back to the Future" theme, featuring all of Johnny's "hit" songs playing in the background. Johnny is happy too, in his own way, jumping up and down as if he is on a pogo stick. That's the sign that he's—to use Mom's word—engaged.

The thing about autistic kids is that they all have their own unique way of being odd. "They are like a box of chocolates," one of the mothers says as she and Mom talk about how different all the boys are, even though they are all autistic.

"You never know what you're going to get," my mother answers back with a smile. She's looking relaxed. It is good to see her like this.

Johnny always had boys in his classes; that's because most autistics kids are boys. And they all have some "thing" that makes each one quirky in his own way. I mean, Johnny's thing is singing classic rock songs. There's this other kid in his class who's obsessed with Steven Spielberg movies. He can tell you everything you ever wanted to know about what year he won an Oscar, the running time of *Schindler's List*, his first student film—that sort of thing.

"Did you see *Close Encounters of the Third Kind*?" he asks me.

"Ah, no," I say, willing to play along, only this kid is serious.

"It was released on November 15, 1977, and starred Richard Dreyfuss, who also starred in an earlier film Steven Spielberg directed called *Jaws*. Did you see *Jaws*?"

"No," I say, trying to find a graceful way to exit. Then I just say, "I've gotta go."

"Okay, it was nice talking to you," he says, as if he's reading from a script.

There is this other kid who sits the whole time with his laptop on his lap, earnestly typing away and announcing his latest find on Hotels.com.

"You can get a king-size bed for only ninety-nine dollars at the Ramada Inn in Tyson's Corner," he says. "Who is going to Tyson's Corner? Are you going to Tyson's Corner?"

"No," I answer.

"Where are you going?" He looks at me excitedly. "Do you like Kansas City? There's lots of good deals in Kansas City."

"Kansas City, Missouri, or Kansas City, Kansas?" I ask him.

"Missouri. It's Missouri. Here's one at the Best Western with a suite for four and a free continental breakfast. It also has an indoor pool—"

"That's nice."

"They have a late check-in time, as well, if you need it."

"Thanks," I say, trying to make a graceful exit.

"I'm going to check Kansas City, Kansas, as well, now that you mention it." He starts typing and clicking away. This kid won't let up. He can go on all night like this.

"Well, that's an interesting place, Kansas City," I remark as he scrolls down the list of great deals on hotel rooms. I realize he isn't really interested in what I think. It's like all those specialists say—these kids don't read social cues. Sometimes I wonder if I have some of those traits myself. I mean, I don't want to be known as a bore.

Johnny's friends have normal brothers and sisters who come to the party, as well. It is actually fun hanging out with them. We don't talk about our siblings much, which is good. Once, Mom had me go to this "siblings of special needs kids" workshop when I was about eight, and we all talked about what it was like having a brother or sister with a disability. It was okay. I remember I had fun playing some of the games. But now, we are just talking, and I realize that at least for the moment, I don't have to be embarrassed so much by what Johnny does, because they all have brothers who have their own weird quirks.

Elizabeth is sitting on the sofa in the family room, talking to a girl who turns out to be the sister of the Hotels.com kid.

One kid I even know from history class named Andrew. I didn't know Andrew has a brother like Johnny. When I say "like Johnny," I don't mean exactly like him. His brother, named Philip, is weird in the way that autistic kids are weird. The weird thing he does is saying that everything stinks. And saying it really loud. In fact, every word that comes out of the kid's mouth is like a bullet shooting out of a machine gun.

"Hey! Do you like Grand Theft Auto?" Philip shouts at me like a drill sergeant.

"I don't play that game," I tell him calmly.

"Why?" he shoots back.

"Because I like to play Call of Duty."

"I don't play that game. I bet it stinks."

"Yeah, I guess it stinks," I say. Andrew just laughs.

"That's what you have to do to get him off your back," he says. "Just agree that whatever he says stinks, stinks."

Then their mother puts her hand on Mom's shoulder and explains, "I have June here to thank for cleaning up Philip's language," she gushes about the teacher, Ms. Smith.

"Oh, it's nothing." Ms. Smith waves off the compliment.

"No, seriously!" she insists. "Before he entered your class, Philip used to say everything was blanked up. Oh my God, I don't know where he learned to use all that profanity, but he had the filthiest mouth!" She puts her arm around Ms. Smith's shoulder. "But thanks to June, now everything just stinks!"

"Well." Ms. Smith smiles, looking slightly perplexed at the compliment. Mom just laughs. Philip searches for another victim, and he finds one in the teaching assistant.

"Hey, Mrs. Porter!" he barks. "Your hair. Did you get it cut?"

"Yes, Philip, I did." Mrs. Porter smiles at him, cupping a hand on the side of her head.

"Well, it stinks!"

Everyone laughs, including Mrs. Porter, but Ms. Smith scolds him.

"Philip, that's not an appropriate remark! You apologize right now to Mrs. Porter."

Philip stands there, looking as if he's trying to understand why his remark was inappropriate. "Okay, Ms. Smith, I'll do that, but I don't understand. I thought I was just stating a fact."

"Philip!" Ms. Smith tries to steady her voice from sounding too annoyed. "We've talked about the difference between fact and opinion. Remember?"

"Anything that stinks is just my opinion," Philip says, speaking in a rote tone.

Ms. Smith nods. "That's right, Philip."

Philip goes back to the teaching assistant and starts taking deep breaths. "Mrs. Porter. I. Am. Sorry! I forgot that my opinion is not a fact."

"It's okay, Philip," she assures him. "Don't worry. My hair will grow back."

"Good!" he yells. "Because I want the old Mrs. Porter back!"

Everyone goes over to Mrs. Porter to assure her that her new haircut looks nice and not to pay any attention to Philip. After all, he's autistic.

"I knew she cut it too short," Mrs. Porter says fretfully.

Mom is laughing a lot. She and Dad are talking with all the other parents and the teachers. She looks younger when she smiles. I wish she could always look this way.

It gets really hot very early in the mornings these days in Adele. We have to get up at around six thirty to eat breakfast, take a shower, and get ourselves dressed, as well as help make sure Johnny is properly dressed. I make sure the buttons are buttoned correctly. And Dad ties his tie. Mom makes sure his face is really washed off and the fruit drink he likes to have for breakfast isn't a mustache.

The ceremony begins at nine, and the graduates have to be there at eight. I escort Johnny to his classroom, where he and Philip, the only other kid in their class who is graduating this year, will be waiting until it's time to march. I don't mind waiting around here—better to stick around where it's nice and air-conditioned than to have to save a place for everybody in the stands.

As if she read my mind, I get a text from Mom telling me to go to the stands to save some spots closer to where the stage is. "Well, good luck, Johnny." I pat him on the back before taking off. He starts pacing around the room nervously, alternating between hopping, walking, and running.

"It's okay, Johnny," Ms. Smith tries to calm him down.

"Should I stay here?" I ask.

"Oh, no," she dismisses my worries. "We're okay with him. Besides, it's better he spend his energy out here than out there."

"True," I say. "Well, good luck," I say to no one in particular.

As I get to the entrance gate going into the football stadium, I hear a girl's voice calling out my name. "Ben! Ben!" It has a distinctive sound, and I start looking around to find the owner. Finally to my left nearer the concession stand, I see a girl waving at me, smiling and full of energy. I wave back halfheartedly, still not sure who it is.

"Ben!" She runs up to me. "Long time no see! How are you?"

I'm beaming from surprise that such a nice-looking girl would know me. And not only does it appear she knows me; she seems so enthusiastic about seeing me. I'm trying for the life of me to figure out where and how I know her.

"I'm doing great!" I nod my head like I'm a bobblehead and try to cover up my confusion. "So what have you been up to lately?" *Good save, Ben.*

"I'm doing awesome, Ben, and I owe it all to you!" She smiles and looks at me with big eyes, as if I'm her hero. Then I figure it out.

"What do you owe me, Melissa?" It is Melissa, minus the excess oil and fat. Plus, she is wearing a skirt, showing off some nice-looking legs. After a few seconds I realize I'm staring at her partly because of the shock of the transformation and partly because she really does look pretty.

"What do I owe you?" She repeats my question and looks at me like I'm a rock star. "How about my life! I took your advice about detoxing myself, looking at myself as my own self-contained environmental disaster. And I said to myself, 'Melissa, we've got to work on you, clean you up, girl!'"

"Well," I say slowly, trying to sound kind, "you weren't a mess, Melissa." Although of course she was.

"I was, Ben!" she insists. "So I cleaned up my insides. And my outsides."

"Oh, nice." I make a face that says, "Spare me the details," but she doesn't get it and goes full speed ahead.

"I did a colon cleanse at first, which was, talk about an environmental disaster!"

"Oh, yeah, I bet." I grit my teeth in a smile.

"So then," she proceeds like she's selling her secrets on her own infomercial, "I go back to the basics. I just start the process of dumping: dumping sugar, dumping processed foods ..."

At this point, I'm still thinking maybe I could like the new Melissa. She's certainly better-looking than the old Melissa. I'm also thinking, *If she could just shut her mouth every once in a while!*

"I'm really happy for you, Melissa!"

"And then I started adding exercise," she continues without skipping a beat, "which I think of as just movement. I started *moving* more, Ben!" She makes circling motions with her arms as she talks.

"That's good, Mel—"

"First, it was just going on walks. Then I started adding Zumba classes, if you can believe it!" Melissa smiles proudly.

"Yeah" is all the input I can get in the conversation. I'm still smiling on the outside as she rattles off her "movement" routines.

"I'm no longer just an armchair advocate for the environment, Ben," she continues. "I'm not just picking up a little trash down by the river. I'm in the river! I'm kayaking. I'm getting wet. I'm having fun!"

"I think that's great!" I'm also thinking maybe we can rekindle our friendship, which was really an acquaintanceship, but still. I need to find someone to help me get over Emily. Melissa may be just what I need right now, someone who likes me, although to be honest, I find her a tad bit grating. Still, with the way she looks now, I can see myself making people a little envious having an attractive girl by my side. I would just need to figure out a way to curtail the blather.

"So I'm living proof that we can all change if we want to," she summarizes. "That's what's wrong with people these days. They don't move! They just sit on the couch all day!"

"Yeah, well, I'm happy for you, Melissa," I say, and I really mean it.

Just as Melissa starts up about the miracle of coconut oil on sensitive skin, this kid trots up toward us from the men's restrooms. He's looking serious, maybe slightly irritated. He's a slightly built kind of guy, with dark hair and fair skin—not exactly the athletic type by the way he moves. I'm guessing he's more like the kind who would be happy to let his girl make all the moves. Then I recognize him from my freshman science class, though I can't remember his name.

"Hi, Melissa!" He stands right next to her, putting his arm around her shoulders.

"Oh, Brad!" She smiles. "This is Ben. We were in English class together in our sophomore year. Ben, this is my boyfriend, Brad."

"Hi," I say, and he says hi back. Well, I guess asking Melissa out is out of the question.

"Well, this will be us next year," Melissa says, gesturing to the rows of folding chairs on the football field. "I'm getting senioritis already!"

"Yeah." Brad nods. We're all quiet for a moment. Then I remember I'm supposed to be saving seats.

"Well, my brother's graduating today, and I have to find my family," I tell her and Brad. "I better go. It was great seeing you, Melissa."

"Yeah, Ben," she almost gushes. "Maybe we'll be in a class together next year." She looks at me with those puppy dog eyes, which look bigger now that the rest of her face is so much smaller.

"You never know!" I smile back before I make my final exit. "It is good seeing you, Melissa!"

"You too, Ben!" She looks at me longingly, that look girls give only in chick flicks.

It is just as well I didn't share that I wasn't planning on coming back to North Central for my senior year. What would the point be? I take Melissa's new status as an attached girl as another indication that I need to move on. North Central worked out well for Melissa but not for me.

I don't get the prime seats in the bleachers; I get seats closer to the middle. If we look straight ahead, we are in line with the last row of graduates. That turns out to be prime for us, because when all the grads march out, Johnny and Phillip are the last to walk on. Ms. Smith and her assistant walk out by their sides, dressed in gowns, as well, sort of acting as bodyguards, dressing to blend in but ready to pounce when or if anything goes askew.

It is a little awkward going to Johnny's graduation, seeing as I probably won't be here next year. All the memories, even some good ones, small though they are, come back to me. Like that girl, Talia, who sat behind me in calculus class and told me how I looked good in that snapshot with Rosie in the infamous Blake/Marty incident. She's been very friendly with me ever since, making small talk. But that's as far as it got. No use thinking about next year and if I will see her again. I won't be here.

"Make sure you have the camera on zoom when Johnny gets up there," Mom reminds Dad.

"Got it," Dad says as he fiddles with the camera.

As I watch the senior class come onto the field to the sounds of "Pomp and Circumstance" over the loudspeaker, part of me wants to be a part of that brigade of caps and gowns with the school's colors. But I've always felt like an outsider, and nothing can change that.

The graduation ceremony is something out of the playbook of a halftime show at a football game. There is a reduced band and chorus for entertainment and to perform the national anthem. The graduates are, of course, the main event. North Central is a pretty big high school, and there are hundreds of graduates walking in a line. At the very end of the line are Johnny and Phillip, the two graduates from the autism class, escorted by Ms. Smith and Mrs. Porter.

After a couple of opening remarks from the principal and other school administrators, Dr. Hemphill gets up again and introduces the next act as "a tribute to our fantastic graduates." Then this girl from the chorus starts singing like Beyoncé (or rather like Beyoncé if someone is choking her). Everyone else is cringing. Mom and I look at each other like *WTH?* Dad gives a look like he just stepped in dog poop. The choral group caps it off with this song from some boy band, and they sing it a cappella.

"Oh my God, this stinks! It really stinks!" Phillip yells. Unfortunately, the wind carries Phillip's voice better than the sound system. People in the stands are chuckling at his critique.

"Be patient," Ms. Smith admonishes.

"Oh, the humanity!" he wails.

"Phillip, be quiet!" Mrs. Porter says sharply.

Ms. Smith and Mrs. Porter hover over him, trying to be as discreet as possible, but it isn't working. Phillip, Ms. Smith, and Mrs. Porter are quite a sideshow—better than the show that was rehearsed!

"Just a little while longer! Sshhh! It'll be over soon!"

"Cut to the chase, and get on with this, for the love of God!" Philip gripes.

Poor Phillip. He is just saying what everyone else is thinking. That's one advantage to being autistic: no one can get too upset with you when you blurt out the truth. After all, it's part of the disability.

Dr. Hemphill, the principal, goes up to the mic and says, "Now, wasn't that lovely?" Like he really means it. Either he's being extremely kind or he is totally tone-deaf.

At least Johnny is behaving himself … until he gets up on the stage to accept his "diploma." Johnny and Phillip are among the first to get their diplomas. The plan was that they would get their diplomas and be whisked away before any more disturbances could occur.

"John Steven McDowell," Mr. Strong announces as Johnny's comes to receive his special diploma. It all seems to go according to plan.

Then Johnny has to make his contribution. As he steps up to shake Dr. Hemphill's hand, he looks out at everyone and makes that goofy smile he does when he's going to do something embarrassing. Then he takes Dr. Hemphill's hand that's holding the microphone, steers it to his mouth, and starts singing.

"Don't let me down! Don't let me down!"

I see Dr. Hemphill trying to gently pull the mic away, but Johnny won't stop. He grips Dr. Hemphill's hand tighter and gets louder.

"Don't let me down! Don't let me down!"

There's an air of tension in the crowd and then some murmuring.

Holy crap, Johnny! Don't do this! I'm thinking as I grit my teeth.

Dr. Hemphill just smiles and shares the microphone. "Ah, who remembers the Beatles? Come on, I'm not the only one who remembers." And then he starts singing, "Don't let me down! Don't let me down!"

And then the chorus teachers starts in and gets the choir to sing. The Beyoncé wannabe really starts belting it out. Soon, the whole graduation class starts singing and swaying.

"Don't let me down! Don't let me down!"

"We won't let you down, Johnny!" he tells Johnny as he hands him a diploma and shakes his hand. As if to let out a big sigh of relief, the crowd applauds.

"Well, that was *different!*" This lady sitting in front of us half laughs and half looks confused, turning around to get affirmation for her opinion.

"Yeah." This man sitting a few seats from us laughs. "Ya gotta keep it interesting!"

None of us—Dad, Mom, Elizabeth, or I—acknowledge that that "graduate" is a member of our family. But I whisper to Mom, "Well, Mom, at least he got everybody singing!"

She looks at me, smiles, and gives me a hug.

Chapter 25

Two weeks after graduation day, so much feels different now that I'm moving on. And yet it doesn't really feel any better. To be honest, knowing I'm going on to a different school doesn't feel that great. What would be great is taking some courses in summer school and graduating early so I can really move on. I don't know. I just wish I could get out of here. Get out of this house. Get out of this stupid town.

I did manage, through J. T., to get a part-time job working with this two-man moving company. Mom is happy with that, happy that I am earning my own money, and I have to admit that it does feel good. Dad is concerned that I will hurt my back.

"Be sure not to bend from the waist. Don't lift heavy objects by yourself," he admonishes.

"Dad, I'm okay. I'm a big boy now."

"Maybe you can go to work for me," he suggests, although realistically, it would take too long to train me for what he would need me to do.

To be honest, I am a little concerned about my back, as well. Not to be a wuss or anything, but if I throw my back out, that will be it as far as a scholarship. But then, I look at J. T. and think he's not worried about his back. I need to be more like J. T. and lighten up.

I am determined to keep my mind occupied enough not to let myself get down. Elizabeth and I have made a pact to keep each other from getting too focused on ourselves.

But the morning of my first move, I get to the location and see J. T. and a two other guys. We say a quick hello and start taking boxes out to the truck.

"Don't mess with this guy," J. T. tells these guys, whose names are Jeff and Fred. "He brought down Blake."

"Blake Barker?" Jeff asks. "Hey, are you the one with the dog who humped Blake?"

"That's Ben!" J. T. beams, like he's proud he knows me.

"Yeah, that's my dog, Marty," I add rather sheepishly.

"But you took him down," Jeff says. "Good for you! I knew that kid back when we were freshmen. Couldn't stand him."

"You know he's going to JMU?" Fred adds as he duct-tapes a box. "He's supposed to be going into political science, same as me."

"It's a big school." I'm stacking boxes to roll away to the truck. "You probably won't even see him."

"Well, Ben, I laughed my ass off when I saw your dog get on that punk," Jeff says as he helps me steady the boxes. "That was great!"

"I'm just glad I won't have to deal with him next year." I shrug off the compliment. But inside I'm beaming more than J. T. is. I'm getting respect. It feels good.

I am icing my hamstring on the sofa when Mom comes in with Rosie through the garage door. She has just taken her to the vet.

"I need to talk to everyone," she says. She sounds shocked. "Keith! Elizabeth!" Mom calls up the stairway. "Oh, Elizabeth is babysitting. I want everyone to be here as a family. We need to talk."

A pain that starts in my chest spreads throughout my body. I don't want to hear what she has to say, but I can't stand the suspense. "It's treatable, right?" I just want to get that answered.

"Just wait, Benjamin," Mom answers weakly. "I don't want to have to keep saying the same thing over and over. Rosie is resting in the sunroom. Why don't you give her a hug?"

I hear the side door opening and turn to see Dad walking in with Johnny and Marty, apparently having gone for a walk. He sees Mom and realizes something's wrong. She runs into his arms.

"I'm sorry, honey." Dad wraps his arms around her. The sound of the garage door opening means Elizabeth has just been dropped off. When she comes in, Mom tells her we are going to have a family meeting in the family room. A look of dread comes over her face.

"Oh no!" Elizabeth starts the cry fest. Unless you have a dog, you won't understand. Rosie is family. She's just a different species.

As we gather in the big room, Rosie gets up, moves into the room with us, and does her spin around before she plops down on the carpet. Marty realizes he's alone and comes into the family room, planting himself in the corner near the window.

Mom takes a deep breath. "You know how Rosie has been rubbing her head against things lately?"

"Yeah, but she's always had allergies." I start to get a sick feeling in my stomach. "I know it's gotten worse."

"Well"—Mom's voice cracks—"Rosie has a tumor. The vet said it's cancer. She's got a tumor around her neck. The good thing is, it's small right now so we got it early."

"So that's good, right?" I ask.

Mom looks hopeful. "He did say that they could operate and do radiation therapy, like they do with people. It's treatable. That's the good news. It's treatable." She takes in a few breaths. "But it's very expensive. Very expensive."

"How expensive?" Dad asks. Now that he has his new business up and running, he's been more aware of the bottom line, asking about the cost of things. Before I got this job, money really didn't mean very much to me. Numbers were abstract. Not so much anymore now that it's my money.

"Over five thousand dollars." Mom closes her eyes. "We have to go to a specialist, a dog oncologist, and I don't know. He gave a list of all the procedures and their costs." She heaves a big sigh, trying not to cry. I'm at a loss as to how I feel.

"That's a lot." I say the obvious.

"Yeah." Mom goes over to Rosie and puts her head in her lap.

"But we have to do all we can for Rosie." Elizabeth starts weeping again. "We can't put her down! Not yet!"

"Don't worry, sweetheart"—Dad puts his arm around her—"we're going to take care of Rosie. We're going to make sure she gets the best treatment out there. We all love Rosie and want her around for a long time."

"Y'all quit talkin' like Ah'm already dead!" Rosie's tail thumps the floor, and everyone smiles. *"Ah'll let y'all know when the time comes."*

"When will that be, Rosie?" Elizabeth falls to the floor on her knees and pets Rosie.

"Ah will tell you with mah eyes." Mom looks into Rosie's face. "She's still got some living to do." She thinks for a few seconds. "But we have to face the fact that she's old, and even without the cancer diagnosis, she doesn't have a lot of years left."

"She's given us some good times," Dad says with a tremble in his voice. Johnny sits at the end of the sofa, as passively as ever. I'm not sure if any of this registers with him.

Elizabeth goes up into her room, and Mom heads into the kitchen to start dinner. Dad tells me he needs to do some rethinking about my going to All Saints in light of Rosie's condition. "I hate to renege on you. And I got the coach there all excited about you going but ..."

"Really, Dad, it's okay. Don't worry about me. I can survive one more year at North Central." I tell him about what Jeff said today about Blake and how I've earned a certain amount of respect there.

"That's good, son. I'm proud of you," he says and gets up. "I have to go down to my office and do a little more work."

"Sounds like this new job is keeping you busy, Dad," I say as I follow him down the stairs. I want to catch the highlights of the baseball games and text Seth and some other guys about their thoughts about the teams.

He turns to me and says, "I know how it is, son, wanting to get out of a situation I feel stifled in. That's how it's been for me for a long time. But I'm starting my own business, with my partners. It's kind of scary. But you know what? I think I needed to be in those places I've been in. They taught me things. I think that's the way it will be for you next year at North Central."

"Yeah, Dad." I smile halfheartedly.

After supper, Dad goes to his office to do some work on his computer. Mom is sitting out on the deck with the dogs lying on the floor near the railing. I step outside and take a seat next to her. "Hi." She looks at me affectionately.

"Hi," I say. We sit in silence, just looking out at the trees in our backyard. We were never big backyard-type people. The backyard has always belonged to Rosie, a place where she could relieve herself and chase squirrels up the trees. It's still light out, and the air is breezy and cool for a summer evening.

Mom and I are still in our thoughts when Johnny opens the door from the sunroom and stands there for a second. Then he screams, "Momma!" He starts crying like a little kid.

Mom runs over and wraps her arms around him. "It's okay, Johnny! It's okay!" She holds him for a moment and then takes him over to the corner where there's a swing chair she got for him to sit in. Johnny has always liked to swing. "Rosie's okay, Johnny. She'll be okay."

I try to be helpful. "Can I get his iPod? Johnny, do you want your iPod?"

"iPod? Yes," he answers.

I come back with his iPod and hand it to him. He unwraps the wires of the earbuds and puts them into his ears. "Fly," he says. "Fly!"

"What's he saying?" I ask Mom. "Fly?"

"Johnny, what song do you want?" Mom asks. "There's no song called 'Fly.'"

This is another instance when Johnny gets frustrating. He asks for a song that doesn't exist, or he doesn't know the name of it. So Mom works with him. "Sing part of the song, Johnny," she'll coach him. "Fly! Fly!" After several attempts, Johnny finally starts singing with her. "Blackbird, fly!"

"He wants Blackbird." She sighs after playing Johnny's version of *Name That Tune.*

"I never heard of that song," I tell Mom as I set the iPod to that song. After Johnny is placated, I sit next to Mom. She's looking wistfully out into the trees in the backyard. She starts singing the "Blackbird" song, something about taking broken wings and learning to fly. "You were only waiting for this moment to arise." She looks at me and smiles. "You were only waiting for this moment to arise."

We sit in silence for a moment.

"I'm sorry about you having to go back to North Central." She looks at me, genuinely sad about the situation. "And having to spend one more year in this house. I know you want to get away."

"It's all right, Mom. Besides, you were the one who couldn't wait for me to get out!"

"I can wait, sweetheart," she says pensively. "That time will come soon enough. But that time needs to come, you know, that time when you need to be on your own." I nod and she continues.

"I just know that you must be a little disappointed that you could have been the top athlete there at that private school."

"Yeah, a big fish in a small pond." I shrug, thinking about what might have been. "I wouldn't have minded that. But I know it's expensive."

"It's just that now with insurance costs so high, you know with your father having his own firm, we have to have a buffer, in case some other unforeseen thing happens. Like this"—she tips her head over toward Rosie.

"Too bad Rosie can't get on Obamacare," I say, trying to add a little humor to our conversation.

Mom turns and gives me a scornful look. "If Rosie were on Obamacare, they'd give her the Old Yeller treatment!"

"The Old Yeller treatment?" I ask her with a blank look on my face.

"Uh-hum." She nods with a sinister look on her face. "You know!"

"No!" I scrunch my forehead. "What?"

"You don't know what happened to Old Yeller?" Mom asks me with alarm.

"I never saw the ending, remember?" I laugh.

"But you must have seen it since then!" She looks at me with an open mouth.

"Mom, that's an old kids' movie," I scoff. "I outgrew it."

"No one ever outgrows Old Yeller!" Mom says.

"Okay. So whatever happened to Old Yeller?" I ask.

"Let's just say Old Yeller went out with a big bang," Mom says slyly.

"Anyway, Rosie will be okay," I say decisively. "Veterinary medicine has come a long way since Old Yeller's time."

"There aren't any guarantees, Benjamin," she tells me, trying to keep me from getting my hopes up too high. "Even if they do operate and Rosie comes out of it okay, she's still an old dog. Every day with her is borrowed time." She walks over and takes Rosie's neck in her hands and buries her face in her muzzle.

I put my arm around her shoulders. "She'll pull through, Mom. Rosie's a strong dog. Don't cry. "Ah jes want mah human momma to be happy!" I tease.

Mom sits up and looks at Rosie sadly. "We just have to prepare for the worst. It is never easy to say good-bye."

I nod sadly at this assessment. No guarantees. But that's life. I imagine Emily saying that she hates that phrase. Well, that's the DNA of life, a series of clichés forming millions of unique combinations.

The door opens, and Elizabeth comes out.

"Hi, sweetheart." Mom extends her arm for a hug, and my sister goes over and gives her a side hug and sits on the end of the lounge chair facing us. "You doing okay?"

Elizabeth has a solemn look on her face. "I'm thinking of creating a dance to show to Miss Rosemary. It'll be a dance in honor of Rosie."

Mom sputters, trying not to keep herself from bursting out laughing. I start grinning too, but I'm not sure where she's going in her head.

"Why are you laughing?" Elizabeth says as she looks at us, becoming irate. "It's not funny. Rosie is dying!"

"I'm sorry, Elizabeth." She covers her mouth and coughs to hold herself in. "What are you going to call it, 'The Muttcracker'!" She looks at me, and we burst out laughing.

"Stop it!" Elizabeth glares at us.

"You'll have to use the leg lift step!" I crack as I stand up and do a series of leg lifts, fire hydrant style. Mom and I start laughing again.

"Stop it, you two!" Elizabeth runs over and slaps me. She is incensed now. "You're not even doing it right, Benjamin!"

"Sorry, honey." Mom tries to get serious. "That's very touching, a dance for Rosie. But sometimes laughing can help you cope with a situation, that's all."

"Well, dancing is how I cope!" Elizabeth says indignantly.

"I know, Elizabeth," Mom says affectionately.

"I'm sorry, Elizabeth." I try to sound serious. "Can you show us moves you have in mind?"

"Maybe instead of 'Swan Lake' you can have 'Bone Lake' and stick little bones in all the girls' hair buns!" Mom chuckles.

"And wear dog collars around their neck!" I add.

Elizabeth is not amused. She stands up and leaves in a huff but not before giving us both a swipe on the knees. "You are both Neanderthals!" She slams the door to underscore her sentiments. Mom and I let our snickers subside before we settle in again.

"It's just as well I stay at North Central anyway." I put my hand on Mom's shoulder. "Who knows if I would have fit in with All Saints anyway? Maybe the kids there would be jerks. Just because it's a religious school doesn't make it necessarily a nicer school."

"Maybe you're right." Mom smiles halfheartedly. "And North Central will be different next year. No Blake, at least."

"Yeah, but I need to smooth things out with the principal now that I'm going back." I look ruefully at her. But she gives me an encouraging look.

"He should look at you with admiration," she says firmly. "You stood up for yourself and for other kids who are—I hate using this word, it's so overused, but—bullied. You showed him what it's like. If he doesn't respect you for sticking up for yourself, then he's an idiot."

"Thanks, Mom." Normally I get annoyed by parents who are constantly taking their kids' side on everything. It happens sometimes in wrestling, when a kid's parent—usually a father— starts arguing with the ref about a call that's against their precious kid. But I'm glad my mother is sticking up for me. Mostly, I'm glad she respects me.

"You look frustrated," she tells me as she curls her legs up. "What are you thinking about?" I shift around in my seat, wishing I could put what is going inside me into words. "What do you want?" she prods. "Use your words."

How can I tell her all that I want? I want to get away, be on my own, be a big success, make my family proud, and make everyone else feel jealous. I want to travel and fall in love with someone who will love me forever. In short, I want my life to mean something. But the words can't come out.

"Ah jes want mah human puppy to be happy!" I say, looking over at Rosie with a smile. Rosie lifts her head and opens her mouth in a smile. Mom looks at her adoringly. "Do you believe that dogs have an afterlife?" I ask her.

"I don't know about *that*." Mom arches her eyebrows. "I do know there's life after high school." Marty, who has been sleeping a few feet away from Rosie, decides to get up. He gives Rosie a gentle nudge on the snout. "I think Marty needs to go for a walk," Mom says and starts to get up. "Do you want to come for a short one?"

"Do you think Rosie's up for a walk? Just a short one?" I want to include her too, but she looks too tired. Mom gives me a doubtful look. "She needs to rest. And I think Marty needs to learn to go by himself sometimes." She gives him a pat on the shoulder and extends her arm out to me.

"Come on," she says with a wry expression, "we can talk about the afterlife of dogs and other deep thoughts."

I add, "And maybe even come up with a little dance!"

Look out for Dogs Don't Wrestle. Coming soon!

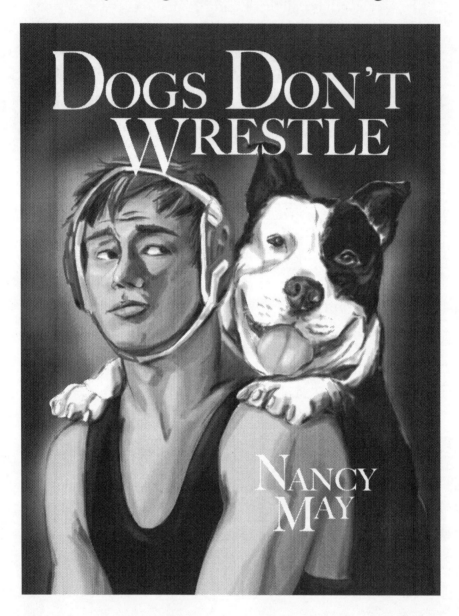